THE BARON ROGUE

AARON COOK

DEDICATION

Dedicated in honor and memory of my grandfathers,

Frederick John Cook

1932 - 2012.

Veteran, Korean War

Rex Lavern Copeland

1922 - 1998.

Veteran, World War II

Thank you for your service.

Always in our hearts.

Gone, but never forgotten.

CONTENTS

PROLOGUE

In the meeting room of J. R. Oppenheimer, there was but one question pacing through the minds of all the scientists that were there: When? Say the word; it will be done. All around the same eagerness was shared, but perhaps the same level of determination was scarce. Not for young Dr. Edward "Eddy" Malcolm, who has been selected by Oppenheimer himself to present the first debut of the models for the atomic bomb. This was by private notification, naturally, so Malcolm's colleagues were unaware of this decision.

Back in his own terminal at home, he installs the last component into his second prototype of the atomic bomb model for the Manhattan Project. These are the two prototypes that will model the atomic bombs to end the War of wars.

"Names, I need names for them. Clever names really sell the deal." He ponders a moment.

"Aha! I know!" He looks around for a can of red paint. It's off to the side, but not where it should be found.

Of course, nothing else could be expected of this man's habits. He has a way with having an organized mess. In his mind, it is a clear labyrinth. To others, it is a fundamental description of what could be called a catastrophe.

"There you are!" he said to himself. "My brush! Good heavens, where is my brush?" For items that seem to complement each other, perhaps it seemed only natural for him to keep essential items as far apart as he physically could.

"If I were me, I was definitely present when I set them down, but maybe not mentally aware of it all. By circumstance, could I have? Oh, don't tell me I did!" Now, the prototypes are currently being suspended above him by less-than-ideal chains.

This man stands about 5-foot-10. These models have a clearance of three feet. It is adjustable, if done right, so as to lower the model to waist height if need be. This would be done when it is finished and ready for transport. They are heavy enough to crack a skull and more, but that didn't phase this mad doctor. He was certain in his ruse.

Make no mistake: these models have no payload yet; they are mere casings, so we can eliminate that weight.

"Of course, I would place my paintbrush across from the prototype, exactly where I cannot reach! Oh, they'll be here any minute! I have to finish this! I mean, they picked me after all to do this project. I cannot fail their confidence in me!"

He sees the paintbrush. Between the brush and him is the larger prototype, spanning about 8 feet. It is convex on one end, gradually narrowing as it approaches the other end, then diverging into a tetrahedral pyramidal shape on that end. He looks up at his project.

"If this chain does not hold, my best chances lie in being hit by the narrowest region." He crouches and steps under the prototype. He shuffles to the other side and grabs his paintbrush. "I most definitely over-thought that. What was I even worried about? There was no w--"

"Greetings, Doctor Malcolm!" bellowed a voice. The door across the opposite side of the room slams wide open. The chains of the model are rattled.

"Oh, hello there, hello! Hi! And please, my son is Doctor Malcolm. I am just a lowly professor," said Malcolm.

"Everything alright, Professor?" asked Armstrong.

"Quite! Everything is tame, I'm just adding finishing touches. You know me, I like adding my own personal flare!" said Malcolm.

"How true of you, Malcolm, how true! Will she be ready then today?" asked Armstrong.

"She is ready right now, even! Would you help me finish these last touches, Mr. Armstrong?" asked Malcolm.

"It would be my pleasure!" exclaimed Armstrong. He hangs his coat on the nearby hall tree. He sees a typewritten note on the workbench next to it. He reads it to himself:

"Dear Dr. Malcolm, It seems that we need my models expedited. We assure you the money will be well worth your trouble. However, do not rush completion if they are not functional in their schematics. Iron out those equations! Everything needs to be balanced. Please re-read that last sentence. We know you just might overlook it. The man with the best design will be my right-hand man in personally silencing the world with this ungodly evil. Yours truly, J.R. Oppenheimer"

"Why would Oppenheimer himself send this? He has his own models." Armstrong thought to himself. "He fathered the idea of the atomic bomb. If this is the case, where was my letter? I am a perfectly capable physicist! No, this isn't right." He walks over to the prototype on the side away from Professor Malcolm.

"Say, Professor, what were these models for again?"

"Oh, ole Oppenheimer was looking for some sketches, but I decided to go all out! I don't see myself as a mad artist, yet the madness flows nonetheless. Perhaps I should embrace it."

"Yes, you should. Do embrace it. It will be your closest companion." Armstrong's voice trails off.

"I beg pardon, Mr. Armstrong?"

"Oh, it was nothing, just some mindless chatter of mine. You know me."

"Well, carry on. Would you mind watching the chain while I come back underneath? In my ignorance, I placed my brush in the worst of places.

"Certainly." Armstrong's voice became almost alarmingly firm. He grabs hold of the model with one hand and the chain with his other.

"Alright, here I go." Malcolm ducks under and starts to shuffle but he drops his brush. "Hold on, I dropped the darn thing. One more second!"

"I'm so sorry, Professor."

"Hm? For what?" Malcolm looks back up.

"For this." Armstrong unhooks the two chains on his side by depressing the switch. He closes his eyes. Malcolm tries to jump out but the model falls on him and hits his head in the process. Armstrong walks over to the other prototype and releases it as well. He rolls it over to Dr. Malcolm.

"How could you? Why would you do this, Armstrong? What—" Malcolm coughs hoarsely.

"Why don't you write what you were going to paint, hm?" Armstrong dips the paintbrush in the can of red paint and hands it to Malcolm. It drips all over him. With the strength he has left, he writes this one word on the model on top of him: "Macht." On the other model, he writes: "Okami." He loses his grip from weakness and drops the paintbrush.

"Nicely done, Malcolm. Now the world can know about my designs! What a convenient choice of color, too, might I add!"

"You are a demon straight from Hell! Aghh!" said Malcolm, panting.

"They'll never know the difference." puffed Armstrong. There is a knock at the door. "Come in, quick! Malcolm is hurt!" Malcolm passes out. Three men enter.

"What's happened here?!" exclaimed one.

"I had just walked in when he did it! I saw him reach for that paintbrush and the model fell right on him. He needs medical assistance immediately!" The men converge onto Malcolm and push the model off him.

"Get him to his son Doctor Malcolm now! He should still be in! I'll telephone it in. Go, quick!" One of the men said.

"It's all over for you, Malcolm. I win," said Armstrong to himself, who stayed behind.

They arrive at the hospital. Nurses and nearby personnel clear the path for the patient. Doctor Malcolm, Jr., comes out of his office door. He runs over to the wheeled bed with his incapacitated father. He leads the way.

"Doctor, is there any hope for your father?" "I cannot tell. There is only one procedure that I can try. It has only been performed once before, but to do something I have never done before, I will need to make some adjustments." Dr. Malcolm, Jr., said reluctantly.

"What kind?"

"I'm going to preserve his memory."

"Is that even possible?"

"Don't tell me what's possible, General. I am the surgeon." They take Eddy to his son's operating theater. It is outlined with machines and the latest prototypes of the newest computer. Eddy was situated into the patient table. His son attached a specialized helmet to Eddy's head. Coming out of it were a plethora of wires that connected to a mobile machine on wheels, measuring about 1.5 cubic meters, complete with two very prominent vacuum tube monitors whose connections extended into an outlet in the machine below them.

The left monitor gave readings for vitals and brain wave activity, whereas the monitor on the right displayed what was in Eddy's mind through his helmet. In conjunction, these readings were relayed to a single source that would become the information for the memory chip.

"Nurse!" shouted Dr. Malcolm, Jr., "are we ready? We've got one shot!"

"We are clear over here, Doctor!" she said from across the room as she read the digital charts on the wall.

"Then let's do this." He fires up the mobile machine. Reaching into his white coat pocket, he pulls out the key card and inserts it into the machine. A button changes color from red to green and pops out.

"On my mark, nurse. Pull the lever when I tell you to." The nurse locates the double-shafted lever.

"Ready!" said the nurse. He takes a deep breath in.

"NOW!" He pushes the green button, and at the same moment the nurse pulls the lever. Buzzing and whirring flared up, and humming was heard all around the room. After a brief couple seconds, the mechanical noises quiet to a tolerable volume.

"How is he?" asked the nurse. A vision of what Eddy is seeing in his comatose dream state is being displayed on the monitor.

"It is time to begin. Sweet dreams, father. We will see you soon," said Doctor Malcolm.

CHAPTER I

THE RUN-AWAY

In this new world, Eddy is sitting in his recliner in his living room. A television news channel is playing. After a moment of ponderance and looking around the room, he gets up to get ready to check the morning mail. Another dose of frantic pattering of the heart is taken. In this time of this grand War, this new World War, it is to be expected of young men to receive a letter of recruitment, a call to the draft.

"Is today finally the day?" He thinks to himself. "Free at last, or forever incarcerated? This way, or that?" A moment to reflect.

"No, whatever it may be, my answer is no!" He storms out of his front door in his nightgown (it was too early yet to be out and about the day). Every step toward the mailbox is slower than the last. Anticipation—overwhelming indignation—is it the truth? He reaches for the handle, but his hand freezes from fear.

He is stopped in solemn thought.

"I'll never look forward to checking the day's mail. Always in the back of my mind, it would appear that I should be expecting something. But mark my words, never something I'll ever want to expect!" He pulls the mailbox handle to the sound of a surreal creak and sees the mail tucked inside, all leaning left against the mailbox wall. Eddy reluctantly collects the envelopes. A quick glance at the sender's address. It's from the recruiting office. He begins to tear up.

"I was never prepared for this." He enters his deepest thoughts.

"They say the feelings are fleeting, to come and go, but they made their home inside my soul. Tell me, when will it all end, this nightmare from start to end? Once upon a time, it began. Free me from my own prison cell, it could not end well. No, don't say it's the end. I'll try and try again, be my friend. Don't go, I don't know what to do. Could you stay a while more? For the loneliness still resides. I desperately hide it inside, but you know just as well in what regard I confide. Save the world with one heroic action at a time.

"Delete all the bad, and all that's left is good, right? If there were no good, and you delete all the bad, tell me what I am? Am I simply nothing, yet again? Oh, here we go, again! One more time, resurrect that old passion fire. It doomed me on that day, but here now I will say, 'It will be okay'."

He fumbles with the envelope and opens it, making numb attempts along the way with whatever coordination he has left. He begins to read the order to report for induction.

"The President of the United States to Edward James Malcolm: By virtue of this notice, you are informed to be trained in either naval or land forces to serve for these United States. Subsequently, you will present to this location as follows: Zero Naught, at 7:00 a.m., on the 1st day of July, 1943."

Eddy drops the letter to the ground.

"Each decision ever made, you had one hope all bundled inside one dream. Am I another story in the history books? Delete them. Delete them all!" Eddy acquired a deft cognizance of the circumstance. "I know what I must do now. It is as simple as can be, and they shall never know the difference."

He dashes back inside his house with the envelopes tucked away to his side, hidden in his gown, lest a passerby suspect any on-goings. Eddy finds a pile of paper and begins to scribble notes furiously.

"They will forever regret the day they drove Doctor Edward Malcolm to this level of madness! This War is not over!" Sheet after sheet, he scribbles onward. "I'll find peace of mind when I finally piece this all together!" was his drive. The hours rolled on.

"What do I need? What exactly will free me?" He glanced at the clock. Exactly midnight. "The oil burns away, I see. I am the father of nano-genetic engineering. The solution should be so clear to me, as one and all the same!" Eddy's eyes widened.

"The solution... is to be the same! I will make another just like me to take my place! It is so brilliant! Genius, Malcolm, genius!"

Eddy scratches a few memos.

"My salvation, my sacrifice. You will be my own Isaac." He stammeringly interrupted himself.

"Oh, and one little twist. You will possess all my knowledge, everything I know, except you will know it for war alone. Make us win this war, and you will be the world's hero. Then, freedom will ensue. We will all be unified! Doesn't that sound so promising? I will be so proud of you. Do it for me, do it for all of us. We are all counting on you. Yes, you! The world's sacrifice! Ahahaha!"

And the downward spiraling lycanthropy, as it were, had only begun.

Eddy heads to his basement where he keeps his make-shift laboratory. As Eddy has called it before, it is his place to perform and conduct "experiments without government clearance, permission, or knowledge."

He prepares his apparati and calibrates every nook and cranny to proper specifications, for he cannot afford to make a mistake now. There is no turning back when one avoids the battlefield.

The lights dim: the atmosphere is set. One could even imagine a spotlight and a red carpet.

A figure looms in the enclosed mechanical cylinder, the silhouette tinted by murky fog from the chemical reactions. The door opens from the chamber.

"Tell me, how do you feel?" Eddy calls to it. The figure drudges clumsily forward, as an infant learning to walk.

"I-I feel," the figure replied, "absolutely nothing." Eddy releases a tear of accomplishment.

"Welcome to the family, my one and my own—my equal." Eddy said.

"Yes." The figure stops a second and glances at the floor. "I-I suppose I am."

The figure raises his arms and looks at his hands.

"Do tell me. What is my name, and what is my purpose?" He looks back up toward Eddy, who, with a grin of satisfaction on his face, is slowly rubbing his hands over and under a few times.

"Your name is Edward Malcolm, and your one sole purpose is to be as destructive as possible. Never hold back, and always show your true power. You are power! *Macht*! For I have made you! An uncontestable force to be feared by all!"

"If I am all that you say I am, then I do assume fully warranted control over anything I deem a threat to me. Is this correct?" Macht asked.

"I couldn't have said it better myself, Macht!" Eddy's eyes glisten with unprecedented vitality. "My creation," he thought to himself, "it is so beautiful!"

"When does my mission start, father?" asked Macht.

"You depart tomorrow morning, which is the first of July. Do not worry, I have everything together already for you. It is all according to plan, I mean, to make sure you are fully prepared, that is! Yes, you are prepared for absolute victory!"

"I understand," Macht smirked.

"Ah, you do have emotion. I am well pleased with you." Eddy said. "You will make a fine soldier of war."

"If war I must, then war I will," replied Macht.

"I'd expect nothing less from my little 'Baron Rogue'," said Eddy.

"What is a 'Baron Rogue'?" asked Macht. Eddy contemplated a moment before answering.

"The one who serves his country, no matter the risk or cost, and redeems it for all—a liberator—is the 'Baron Rogue'. And that is your duty that I am sure you will carry out without error," answered Eddy.

"Errors… I know not the meaning. I cannot accomplish what I do not know, only what is my destiny," grinned Macht.

"Y-yes. Precisely!" nervously replied Eddy.

Eddy went to bed that evening in a turmoil of uncertainty. Half past midnight, he awoke in a night sweat after dreaming about Macht at war. Had he done the right thing? Was this truly the right course of action? He stumbled and stuttered over his writhing thoughts and emotions until the heavy guilt put him back to rest. Time alone will tell if these questions are validated.

Time alone is an enemy against all odds, swirling its victims into the whirlpool of choice and consequence. The end is unchangeable. Or, is it, perhaps? Who is brave enough to correct their own actions? That accolade belongs to none other than the Baron Rogue Proper. In the evens and the outs, the ups and the downs, only one remains always and consistently.

That person is the Baron Rogue. Hail, hail, the champion of time-and-again! To the beloved sacrifice never-meant-to-be but always-will, to the soldier who never tasted true victory, to the son that never got to say goodbye, to the Baron Rogue, who is the epitome of this all, you have been unheard and unseen. Be known, be seen, be heard! It is now or never. Never have another regret again. Choose now!

The next morning, Eddy knocked on Macht's door.

"Good morning, my son, are you awake?" No response. Eddy knocked again. Still nothing. He opened the door to find nobody home. Then, Eddy heard a thud coming from the direction of his truck. He peeked out the window to find Macht already packing up to head out. Eddy saw him enter the vehicle ready to go, so he rushed downstairs, grabbed his keys and documents on the counter, and headed out the door. He left behind something he will regret later--a document containing sensitive identity information for when he is to arrive.

Eddy roughly climbed into the truck, staggering in his movements. He checked his watch: 6:30 am. He had slept in for almost a whole hour.

"I am ready, father," said Macht.

"I apologize for my lateness, I had problems sleeping last night, you could say."

"I understand. Sending someone off to war does not seem easy, albeit necessary in these times, huh?" said Macht.

"Absolutely, my son. My equal and the best of all of us."

The drive over to the station was mostly quiet. Macht peered out the window, observing the passing scenery. Eddy had his gaze fixed on the road like a statue. He could not bring himself to look over at him as the guilt gradually built. One question after another: What if Macht doesn't make it home? What if they find out? Does he have everything to fabricate this scheme? Will they buy it?

"Hey, question," popped up Macht.

"Oh, hello, uhh, answer," said Eddy.

"Do tell. As I witness this daylight beaming against the countryside, with how beautiful this scene appears, why is the world so angry and bitter? Do they not see things as I do, as potential for grandeur?" asked Macht.

"If only that were so, but there are those that wish to destroy that which is beautiful. There are those who do whatever it takes to get what...they...want...." Eddy's voice slowed down and trailed off in his answer. He feels increasingly aware of his situation.

"Hm. Quite a shame. To me that is wasteful of what is already in sight, as opposed to what is in future sight. I feel I am left with a split decision. I could spend my days focused on what could be, or I could make use of what already is. And I think that is quite an undertaking to the ungrateful," said Macht.

"My son, you are so wise. Never change this mindset; you will bloom under the hottest fires and the thickest smoke. It is the pressure that creates the diamond, so shine brightly and fiercely," said Eddy.

"I will keep that in mind," said Macht.

Seven-o'-clock. Not a minute sooner or later they arrived. Eddy handed off to Macht what he'd need for drafting. The arched sign above the entryway reads the label "Zero Naught."

"I wish you the best, my son. I am always a letter away if you need someone to talk to," Eddy said as Macht intricately exited out the truck with his effects.

"Always, father. I will not fail in my mission. I hope we see each other again. That is, I can't wait to see you, Eddy." Macht said before closing the truck door and leaving the scene.

Eddy, dumbfounded, left his mouth agape for a few seconds before driving off.

CHAPTER II

WHEN A GOOD MAN GOES TO WAR

"Line up at attention, all of you! Sarge wants to take a good look at you."

The new recruits broke their clique huddles and formed a rather abrasive line in front of the corporal.

"You call this a line? How are you going to shoot straight if you can't think straight? Try again!" disappointedly shouted the corporal.

After another couple bumbled attempts, a straight line was finally managed.

"Better! Alright listen up, and listen well. I will not repeat myself. You are all aware of what happened at Pearl Harbor, I'm sure. We do not make the same mistake twice. The enemy does not care about you, your feelings, or your family. If they want you dead, they will make it happen. If we do not take on a similar mindset, we will all die. Sarge and I will not let that be us. So let me be clear: any one who does NOT give their best will be sent home in utter disgrace, and you can explain to your mommas why SHE RAISED A COWARD! Hooah?!"

"HOOAH!" the platoon exclaimed.

"Ugh, civilians," mumbled the corporal to himself. A half-track pulled up behind the corporal.

"That was a cute battlecry, corporal. I'm afraid we could do better someday. If we are to have the best men, we must have the best spirit." The man stepped down from the half-track.

"Sergeant James! Attention, soldiers! Show your commanding officer some respect!" Sarge treaded up and down the line, each private saluting and staring motionless into the distance. Macht's knees begin to buckle slightly.

"Little wobbly in the knees are we, private? What's your name?" asked Sgt. James. Macht chokes a second, sweat beginning to bead down his face.

"Edward. Edward Malcolm."

"You don't look like an Edward, son."

"It's my... father's name," replied Macht. Sarge returned a blank stare of sarcastic placation, reminiscent of apathy mixed with grief.

"Well, Malcolm, looks like we got some work to do. Everyone, fall in on me!" exclaimed Sarge.

As the days of training turned to weeks, news of the on-going global conflict only strengthened the heart of the American soldiers-in-training. They were eager to give it their all. No matter the cost. On occasion, Macht would journal, penning his thoughts about it all, whatever was on his mind.

"I cannot remember the last time I have received good news. Redact that, I cannot recall ever hearing good news. Will all this struggle bring good news? Do our means actually justify the ends to this abhorrent turmoil? Perhaps I could do something about it. Maybe I could unite instead. If I could get everyone on the same side, then there would be no sides to choose. Yes, everyone could at last be free. Freedom sounds so… free."

Macht's vision turned blurry and doubled. Profuse sweating out of nowhere flooded his face. He closed his eyes and saw burning trees and glass breaking. Suddenly, he suffered intense chest pain and dropped the pen to the floor. He opened his eyes again.

"Hah, what's up this time, Malcolm? Is our little poet all tuckered out from fantasy land?" retorted a fellow comrade. The gratuitous sounds were drowned out in the sea of his thoughts.

Macht collapsed to the ground.

"NURSE!! WE NEED A NURSE OVER HERE!! HEART ATTACK!!" shouted another comrade, unsure of what else to say. Macht awoke in a bed under the canopy of the nurse's tent.

"W-what happened?" he asked the nurse sitting at his bedside.

"A couple of your battle buddies found you on the ground when you were journaling. I checked your heart and vital signs but everything seemed fine," reassured the nurse.

"Hm. Quite a bit of stir for everything to be only fine, huh?" chuckled Malcolm. The nurse giggled back. Macht had a slight deadpan stare at the nurse, his mouth stuck in a half-smile.

"What's your name, miss?" asked Macht.

"You can call me Rebekah, but don't get your hopes up, Malcolm. Can I call you Malcolm?" she asked, after a quick glance at his charts.

"Miss Rebekah, you can call me anything you want, except for Malcolm. Call me Eddy." said Macht. Rebekah put the clipboard-attached charts off to the side on a table.

"Well, how about I call you later, Eddy?" hinted Rebekah, turning back around to look at him, eyebrows and corner of mouth both raised. Sgt. James entered through the tent opening into their ward.

"If you two are finished here, I'd like a situation report."

"Malcolm here was writing in his journal and suffered what it presumed to be a mild stress attack. He's going to need a day of rest, as soon as you can give him, or the next attack may not be as forgiving," said Rebekah.

"Hmph. Malcolm, take the day off tomorrow. We need every man in top-shape for the upcoming theaters, which may as well be called circuses at this point, but no one asked me," said Sarge. The next day found Malcolm alone with his thoughts and his journal again. He must have filled a couple dozen pages, some tear-stained. Among them were penned this page:

"Eddy said I was created to be a man of war and to know only of it. But yesterday I was met with an antithesis yet also a perfectly synergistic match: love is a form of war. I fight for what I love, much like most of my comrades. I fear my stress attack yesterday was an internal conflict between what my molecules dictate as the norm for my body and what my head desires. Does this mean that, if I choose anything besides bloodshed and violence, that I simply fall apart? If I delete all the bad, then does all the good remain? What... has Eddy done to me?" The rest of the page was dampened with teardrops.

After some time to reflect, Macht turned angry with indignation, his countenance even showing so. He turned to the next fresh page and began to draw schematics and mock-up models.

"If a war I must fight, then a war I must win. For you, Rebekah. And for everyone else. And they'll never see it coming. I AM MACHT—The darkness come alive, the harbinger of catastrophe, and the swift end to all things good. If I cannot love, then perhaps no one should."

Drawings, sketches of horrendous weapons and gadgets flooded the rest of the journal. Down to the nth decimal the math flowed like a waterfall, seamlessly connecting all of it.

"What do I need? How do I need it, how is it used?" More and more Macht dove into this train of thought. The more he did, the more energized he felt, for this was his true nature for which he was created. Every new page showed greater inspiration and more promising results. At the very end, it all amalgamated into a simple idea, his own eureka:

"This device to employ, by none other than I, shall be the cold termination of all that oppose my will. This grenade, as it were, will turn friend into foe, and foe into dust. Dust to dust, the principle remains. As it once was, and evermore shall be, let no one be left behind in its wake. My device will steal its victims memories or, worse, turn allies against each other. Maybe it will simply explode and leave nothing in its path of desolation. Heh.

Only it will know, for I do not, until I decide otherwise. For now, this is its beauty. My little 'induced-recruitment or amnesia grenade.' You have so much potential. So compact, yet so powerful. We do have work to do."

The years rolled on. Wars of rumors of wars are ubiquitous and have infested nearly every populated place on the earth.

Macht's journal records these moments:

June 5, 1944.

Bad weather has put off Operation Overlord for some time now. Plans to leave for Normandy effective immediately upon the first report of clear weather.

Tonight, Macht polished his plans for the invasion.

June 6, 1944.

It's time. The day is finally here. In number, our vessels total 6,939. I was on one of the many landing craft. Sgt. James said he wanted me at the front, telling me I'd never make it past 3 feet. So you know what I did? I sought to prove him wrong. Under my uniform, I wore armor that no one else knew about but I. If found out, I'd face a heavy court martial because it's not standard issue, nor do I possess the appropriate rank.

My gun was doctored to carry a magazine of bullets I carefully crafted as well. I figured, if Sarge lives to lecture me, I'll take my chances. These bullets are numbered, each one having a different effect. In the first magazine of 24 rounds, I know exactly what each one can do. First, I fire a concussion round. The next 3 are incendiary. As they deal with the fires, I will shoot the fifth round that will send shrapnel every which way. The ten bullets that follow have exceptional penetrating qualities that will cut through concrete like it's nothing. For the final 9 rounds, each set of 3 has a surprise effect of either incendiary, penetrating, or ricochet. I regret absolutely nothing, for I am this.

"Hey! Be alive and alert, Malcolm! It's go-time!" yelled Sarge.

The beach is in view. You practiced this Macht. One bullet straight ahead, 2 to the left, 1 to the right, then back to middle. After that, it's imagination from there.

"We're here. I countdown the seconds I have for my plan. 10. 9. 8. 7…" "Men," said Sarge,

"Godspeed. For glory, for honor, and for God and country!"

"3. 2…" The landing craft door began its slow descent. Macht waited and counted for that exact moment.

"Now!"

As soon as his eyes were able to peer down the top of the door, he let them have it. The Germans never saw it coming. His allies behind him couldn't believe how quickly the scene unfolded. The bunkers on the beach crumbled into heaps of rubble immediately. Onward they pressed, an onward Macht raced. His relentless chase for glory soon halted.

Macht had strayed onto his own path, soon finding himself at the mercy of the Germans. In that still moment, looking down the barrels of at least a dozen guns, Macht shouted a German phrase: "*Lang lebe das Reich!*"

In their confusion they lowered their weapons briefly but for oh-too-long. A stunning grenade was stowed away on Macht's waist belt. He swiftly tugged it off and hurled it into their midst. Macht drew his gun and scrapped the enemies for hard and good. Into the unknown perils of Normandy Macht delved deeper.

Finally, he had a moment to himself. His thoughts bombarded his mind like cannon shells on a rock-strewn bulwark.

"Maybe, perhaps, I am not so different from those I call 'enemy'. Maybe I am the enemy. But, if I am the enemy, then who is right? I was told that I am doing the right thing by fighting for my country. I struggle with this, for I have no country to call home. Eddy never told me where my home was, what my country even was. I had to find that out during training. I was trained to have a purpose other than my own. They tried to fill my head with all their ideas and ways to kill someone. This cannot be right. In order for me to be right, I have to end the life of those I disagree with, right? What if I disagree with everyone? What if no one is right, if this is how disputes are always settled among men?"

"*Hände hoch!*" shouted a German. Macht chortled lamentingly.

"*Mich einsperren. Ich habe nichts mehr übrig,*" said Macht. Two other Germans appeared and clasped Macht by his uniform.

"Why detain me? I was willingly going with your plans!"

"*Halt dein dreckiges Maul,* American!" they shouted.

"Have it your way, but don't say I didn't make you an offer you couldn't refuse." said Macht.

One of the soldiers stopped and tried jabbing at Macht with the butt of his rifle, but Macht grabbed it and swung the soldier into the other. The third soldier tried to shoot Macht, but he grabbed one of his friends as a shield. Among the shouting, Macht dropped another stun grenade on top of a smoke grenade and made his escape.

"One way or another, I will find a way to return," said Macht to himself. "If I cannot reason with infidels, American or German or whatever ethnicity I am propagandized to hate so lavishly, then I will make them reason. Is this justified? Who knows, but I am beyond asking now."

Macht's self-reflections would have to wait. Five more soldiers showed up, and Macht ultimately surrendered. He was transferred to Germany for trial. Caught with contraband, he was sentenced to a prison in Austria. That was futile and massively short-lived. Macht fled to a small, abandoned cottage to the east of the prison.

In his peaceful dwelling there, he made a plain abode to call home.

As time progressed, word spread that an American outsmarted the unholy prison of the *Anschluss*.

One evening, he was greeted by a knock at the door. Two men appeared before him, one of high-command and the other a messenger. They demanded he go with them. Macht refused, stating he had no more quarrel with the world and its wars. Instead, he desired to pursue his own interests in science.

He believed science was the key to achieving his penultimate goal: global unity achieved through technology. The man of high-command shot his messenger, unironically, and gave up his orders to be Macht's right-hand man.

"So, what do they call you out there on the battlefield?" asked Macht.

"Out there, I am called the 'Wolf of the Axis' or 'Okami,' but back home, in Japan, my name is Yakeru, the all-consuming fire," said Okami.

"Okami, is it? My father calls me Edward Malcolm or Isaac or Macht. But I read about this German word, *Macht*. This I prefer, for I am power. Join me, Okami, so we may rise above the peasantries of war, and ascend to the royalties of science!" exclaimed Macht, arms jubilantly thrown open.

"We shall, indeed. I have heard of this Edward Malcolm guy, because my Emperor told me that he is a part of this collaborative Manhattan Project to develop what are called atomic bombs. So what did you have in mind going forward?" asked Okami. The most gallant of malicious smiles emerged on Macht's face.

"We bring the battlefield to him," said Macht.

CHAPTER III
MIND YOUR BUSINESS

*I*t is now the riveting summer of 1945. Macht was presumed to be MIA in combat since 1944, but made his way back to Eddy unnoticed, although Eddy now only remembers the original name given to Macht, which is Isaac Armstrong. For the past few months, Macht has been serving as an understudy and assistant professor to Eddy, aiding him in research for the Manhattan Project. Select scientists appear at the Los Alamos Laboratory for the final discussion of the Manhattan Project.

The most deadly weapon ever devised by the cruelty of science up to this point in history is being birthed. Only the most brilliant and composed masters of science were able to chance their intuition at researching this magnum opus. Though in total they number 600,000, and some more, the profile of each person, quite confidently, boasts the accolade of surviving a struggle—that is, the struggle for integrity. At this point in world history, it is very much a scarce resource. A world-breaking decision is going to be made today in a *small meeting. Eddy begins his time there by having an exchange with Oppenheimer outside the facility doors.*

"Doctor Edward Malcolm?" inquired Oppenheimer. Eddy nods.

"You can just call me Eddy," replied Eddy.

"Welcome to the Manhattan Project. Doctor J. Robert Oppenheimer—an honor to meet you." He looks over beside him. "Who is your friend?" asked Oppenheimer.

"Professor Isaac Armstrong. He is my assistant," answered Eddy.

"What a brilliant partnership. Do come. The meeting awaits, gentlemen!" invited Oppenheimer.

Doctor Malcolm nods at his assistant to validate his rite of passage. On the occasion, a smile appears on the assistant's face, as one who feels empowered and respected. It could be that he has never had this experience, by the look on his face. If Eddy had the slightest gesture of euphoria, it has dissipated now.

In this conference room, a small group of presumed scientists is seated around the tables. One could tell that these few were selected so particularly and precisely, refined and fine-tuned a thousand-fold over, that if they are not the absolute best at what they do, they should not be here. These giants stand mountains above all others in the sciences, one can conclude. There is hushed mumbling among them. The seat at the front is empty. Everyone is waiting on a single person to commence this meeting to order. It must be Oppenheimer. Eddy believes they underestimate Oppenheimer's understanding. Where could this man be? Being the figure of influence he is, it could be that several persons have stopped him to obtain a small piece of information that shall last their mindset a lifetime. Yet, to him, it was a mere second out of his time.

Eddy's assistant sits eagerly in the corner—and how somber. His face is furrowed in what is guessed to be pensive apprehension. Over what? It couldn't be guessed; but his mouth quivers from silently thinking aloud. A paradox of thought—the most secret portions of a man being published (even in this nearly inaudible fashion) did not bother him. Oppenheimer arrives. He has the room's attention with his presence alone. This is the anticipated man. He takes a moment to collect himself before he sits down. A quick survey of the room—notes are jotted down while everyone else respects the silence. Perhaps it is attendance he is recording, or some profound mental note or last-minute epiphany.

"Welcome, all," Oppenheimer begins. "This officially commences the council for concluding our decisions in the Manhattan Project. A salute to every person represented here. Our achievement could not have been accomplished without your collective, dedicated efforts. America shall be known domestically and globally as an unprecedented force in the history of war.

"We, however, do carefully consider the repercussions our actions shall take. Men, and woman," he gestures to the one young lady scientist present, "we must carry through with utmost dignity for the lives that it shall sever from this earth. The act will surely echo into all following generations. Take your oaths now, good people. This is your last chance to do so."

As the meeting carries on, Professor Armstrong, in his inconspicuous corner, is jotting down notes of his own as well.

Eddy glances over, as he is seated at Armstrong's 10 o'clock, and notices that his assistant is merely scribbling! How could he do this, in such a serious time?

Upon further inspection, Eddy notices that his assistant is not scribbling mindlessly. No—heavens, no—he is furiously writing away like some madman having a revelation by self-acclaimed divine intervention. Eddy knows this experience from his own life. He, too, on his most brilliant occasions, writes in that manner. Oppenheimer at last adjourned the meeting. "Thank you all again for your time and attendance. I will be proud to announce to our overseers that we are ready to, if you will, unleash all hell." On the way out to the vehicle, Eddy keeps a low conversation with his assistant.

"What did you happen to note down?"

"How do you mean?" The assistant questioned.

"I noticed you were writing rather angrily, like you had been struck with the grandest idea. How ironic, in a meeting discussing the most complex invention yet, that you could have that." A chuckle from Armstrong.

"Oh, so you did. It was nothing, really. I had a thought that needed to be recorded at the time," said Macht.

"What kind of thought?" Eddy provoked.

"Hm? It is not important, but I treasure it. Think of it as a journal entry," retreated Macht.

"Fair enough; have it your way," agreed Eddy. Outside the laboratory, the assistant stops Eddy. A vehicle has pulled up.

"Eddy, a moment," said Macht. "I must tell you now, as I have failed to do so earlier: I am required to resume my duties on the battlefield effective immediately. We will not meet for a long while, friend." Shock, disappointment, and sorrow—Eddy is trying to justify this sudden leave. Neither a warning nor notice. How could this be? They had just obtained time to spend together. Eddy had crafted so many plans and experiments that they could have done together. It is a gloomy uprising, as observed when the clouds roll over the sun's gleam to produce an unsettling darkness.

Eddy watches as Armstrong gets inside the vehicle.

"Right this way, Macht." The chauffeur opens his door.

"W-who is this Macht?!" Eddy questioned himself. A steady grin widens on Macht's face. Eddy is overcome with astonishment.

What has just happened? Is there some double life he leads? On the brink of the world's calamity—no, desolation, rather—are they met here so suddenly with a near-reality of internal usurpation?

"What have I done, Eddy?" He stands numb as the automobile drives off with Macht.

"This… isn't good. At all." Eddy strides to his vehicle and drives off, now realizing who that is, and what that is going to mean. Inside the car with Macht and the chauffeur is another person as well.

"Macht," the other passenger began.

"Hello, Okami," said Macht.

"So, what did you learn?" inquired Okami. Macht passes him the notes he jotted down during the conference. It must mean something significant to them—the paper looks like a typographic mosaic.

"This must be what we were needing. Most excellent, Macht," said Okami.

"It was rather easy. I was almost surprised," said Macht.

"Did you-know-who ask about it?"

"He did, but the old man gave up after I brushed him off. Like father, like son."

"Hmph. When do we head out?" asked Okami.

"Tomorrow morning, before the split of dawn," affirmed Macht. "I know exactly where the bombs are stationed."

"I'll be looking forward to it," responded Okami.

"The world will be looking forward to it, my brother," Macht emphasized. A minute of nothingness passed.

"You know what this will do to Eddy, don't you? With his being under the Quebec agreement?"

"It has been my intent since my inception to make a point to Eddy that he will finally see." Macht assured.

It is now the dawn of the next day—August 6, 1945.

At Okami's quarters and hideout, they ready-up the motorcycles. Both Okami and Macht have geared themselves for this moment down to the second, backpacks in hand and immediate essentials on the belt.

"When does the first jeep pass by?"

"In approximately 17 minutes. We must be out this door in exactly 20 seconds."

"Heheh. We are slightly ahead of schedule. Excited are we?"

"That we are. History will be made today. The world will never forget what we are to do." They mount onto the motorcycles.

"Call it, Okami."

". . . Go!" The engines sharply roar. The two of them bolt straightway to the road behind the hideout. Fifteen minutes have passed. They arrived at the first checkpoint.

"Two minutes," whispered Okami to Macht.

"Nice. On my mark, we ride." Okami planted spikes in the road. Macht placed a timed flash device at his spot. They pulled goggles over their heads to brace for the moment of trial. Headlights emerge from the distance. The sound of a jeep can be heard from behind the electric eyes. Along it chugs, and along it… PLOP.

"Sarge, we got a flat! Wonder what we hit?"

"Men, out! Investigate!"

"Squad A, grab flashlights. Squad B, cover us. I'll watch the front." They hustle out from every opening and investigate the perimeter for threats and dangers.

"What'd we hit, A?"

"Some sort of spikes." Rustling was heard on the side of the road.

"AMBUSH!! Look alive, guns up!" Squad B pointed their guns at the noise. Macht's device started hissing, signifying to him and Okami that in 6 seconds it will explode and produce intense acutely-blinding light.

"Get some lights on that sound!" While they were distracted, Macht and Okami sneaked around to the other side of the truck.

Okami buried an IED on either side of the road during the trek. Three, two, one. FLASH.

"ARGH, open fire!!!" Shots went everywhere. Macht and Okami quickly hijacked the unlocked truck and floored it down the road. Before they could radio in the situation, Okami remotely detonated his two devices, leaving behind no witnesses.

"Why are the simple so easily beguiled?" asked Macht almost embarrassingly.

"A fleeting moment and the mind of the simple are the same. Nothing but emptiness."

"True, my friend. What's next on the itinerary?"

"Not much. We just have to enter the base, intercept the radio, open the hangar doors, and get out of there with the loot."

"In how much time?"

"Hmm. About five minutes. Better make it four."

"Give me a real challenge, Okami." The jeep is stopped at the gate. A flashlight brightly greets them. An officer begins to approach the window.

"Macht, do you have it, or do you need to borrow one?"

"I have one, but it's not tested. Stick to the plan." Macht rolls down the window.

"Identification," said the officer.

"You will find my credentials to be exactly what you're looking for." Macht pulls out a specialized instrument from his belt and flashes a quick shutter at the officer's eyes.

"Y-yes. My mistake. Right this way, and Godspeed. I will open the gate for you." The officer walked back to the gate and pressed a button that lifted it. Macht felt an unusual sensation traverse through his body. It felt empowering.

"What did you say you called that again?" asked Okami. "'Induced-recruitment or amnesia grenade' is what I call it. You could call it an "IRAG" for short. It captures the victim's memories, so I can replace their current ones with whatever I wish. For instance, as was the case just now, I can convince them that they are on my side. This was a one-time use device that is the simplest grenade imaginable. The shutter is actually a micro-explosion in the chamber—as simple as an electron jumping energy levels. So minute and so fast that it is comparable to a lightning bolt. Only the observer could ever notice it. Strange, I felt a physical surge of power rise up within my bones when I did that."

"How mischievous yet fascinating," said Okami.

"Yes it seems so. How long now?" asked Macht, still pondering his finding.

"In 30 seconds take a left, followed by a right turn after 12 seconds. The building will be on the right. You will have 2 and a half minutes to intercept communications. I will wait in the jeep. Then, we have exactly only 1 minute to book it to the hangar, a 45 second drive, and use the remaining time to get what we are after," said Okami.

"Let's get this over with. I have an appointment this afternoon, and I want to be there in one piece, preferably," remarked Macht.

"Here it is, coming up in 5 seconds. Park but leave it running."

"Relax, Okami. Sometimes you need to stop and appreciate the foliage," joked Macht. Okami returned a blank glare. Macht exited the jeep and routed himself to the second floor of the communications building.

"Empty. Not a soul here. What's going on that we don't know?" thought Macht to himself. He found the computer systems, inserted his own disk that remotely links the communication station to their hideout and allows sabotage, and fumbled with each bypassed meter, switch, and virtually every perceivably-tactile object.

"Beautiful," he whispered to himself. "I can't believe it is all actually coming together. I can actually win for the first time in my life. I will show you, Eddy, what happens when you extrapolate more than what you could ever imagine. This is war."

Macht returned to the jeep and they drove to the hangar, parking at an angle. Macht and Okami lift up the hangar door to find the planes with the atomic bombs.

"Right where they're supposed to be. Isn't that beautiful?" said Okami.

"You remember where to go, friend?" said Macht.

"I do." replied Okami. Macht and Okami pause and look at each other. A feeling of hesitation chills them, but it is not stronger than their sense of commitment to the hellish task they are about to perform.

"As a reminder, this never happened. We never knew each other, and... I'll see you on the evening news and back at the lab," said Macht.

"See you then, brother." They embrace hands, with their elbows angled, as a farewell salute should this wickedness consume them so soon.

Macht attaches a strange device to the atomic bomb inside the plane. The device has this name etched into it: "Induced Recruitment or Amnesia Grenade." He attaches another to the backside with some wired release mechanism. It could shoot out by the pull of some trigger at the cockpit. He did the same to Okami's plane with the remaining two devices he had with him. They depart separately in the planes with the atomic bombs. Where could they be going with mankind's deadliest weapon, yet to have ever been used on the battlefield? An officer on patrol overheard the engines revving up from the hangar and checked out the scene. But the planes have already been vacated. In horror, his hand trembles as he realizes the situation and loses its clutch on the flashlight that confirmed his suspicion.

"Sergeant James! General! The planes, the bombs are gone!" He cried. "The bombs are gone! This is not a drill! The bombs are gone!" Lights go up all over the station in succession. A captain furiously charges over to verify the situation. They look up to their three o'clock and see the disgust in action.

"Get lights up there! Someone, shoot down those rogue planes!"

"No! They are carrying the bombs, do not engage over our own skies! Follow them to their watery grave!" The captain calls out.

"Get a radio on that. I need men to chase after them. Six gunners, three each. Now! Go!" Six pilots, each with a copilot, man six fighter biplanes.

"Take to the skies, and make their beds in hell!" screamed the Captain. The planes take formation and split three and three after each rogue plane piloted by Macht and Okami. A signal comes into the radio on Macht's plane.

"This is your only warning, pilot. Ground yourself or you'll be shot! This is an order from the United States Air Force!" the voice commands.

Ignoring the order, Macht privately radios to Okami,

"Watch your six. Don't initiate just yet. On my mark, we take them down one at a time."

"Copied that, Macht. Ready on your mark." replied Okami. Did fear ever make its company in the mind of these two men? Afraid not. Fear itself was much too terrified to dare to attempt that. The planes soar closer, the whirring intensifying. Macht and Okami are far enough apart now but within clear signal distance.

Once more, the order is called out,

"Land your planes! We have every right to bring you down!" Macht only chuckled at this. He mocked its gallant effort.

"Okami, now!" Macht told him. They both released an IRAG device on the rear of the plane. Because of the V formation the other pilots took, it stuck to the cockpit window of the middle plane. Three... two... one. Intense light brightened the sky for a brief second. A quick stillness was broken by a thunderous bang that shattered the windows and ruptured the engines of those planes, but not the ones piloted by Macht and Okami because they were ahead of its detonation. The two wing planes were spared, a pair chasing either bomber plane.

Macht turned in his chair to quickly see if his plan had succeeded. He was met with delight to see the last planes changing their courses in the direction of Okami's plane. Okami witnessed the same thing, except vice versa. The planes started shooting at each other. Pieces flew off. Then a wing, and another. Bullets caught the engine and ruptured it. In their crash course, the planes collided, much to the satisfaction of the masterminds that are Macht and Okami. It was the work of the grenades used.

The objective is to flood the victim's hippocampus through ultraphotonic injection through the eyes and burst the person's memory. In its wake, a 'crater' is made, leaving space for the grenade "thrower" to inject a placeholder memory as long as it is done in the miniscule length of time to do it. As Macht described it in his notes, to be exact, the victim's memory is vulnerable for only 0.762 seconds. In that window of time, at least 26% of that person's known memory has to be erased with a minimum of 78.44% success (this in itself, with the current model of the grenade used, has the odds of 1/4 chances of working).

Once that barrier is bypassed, the mechanism responsible for integrating recruitment has to inject the replacement "memory" with, at this point, roughly 0.238 seconds left. If it does not work, the hypnosis, if you will, loses its vivacity and the original memories come back (think of it as a person juggling, and in-between the juggle the event must happen). Thus, the effort would have been lost and there will be a bigger mess to clean up if the process does not work.

"This is Bombardier Alpha to Base: your proselytes have failed," radioed Macht. "They will not be missed, I assure you. Bombardier Alpha over and out forever." The signal cuts off.

The hours of flight roll onward. At last, Macht can see his destination. Okami is elsewhere, yet to be at his, since it will be a greater distance.

Macht is flying over London, England. A British officer catches his plane coming in and immediately attempts to reach it by radio.

"Attention bomber, you are in a restricted air space. Land your plane now!" Oh, as if Macht has not heard that before! He was not phased.

"L-land your plane?" Macht opens the bomb-bay hatch door.

"What are you doing?! Wait, you're an American plane!" This line will be marked forever in history.

"Have a goodnight, 'Great' Britain!" Macht activates the switch to deploy the atomic bomb directly above parliament. His plane reaches a good distance by the time the bomb nears its impact. He can feel it, any second now and it will— Thunder. Blinding light. Hellfire. Smoke as dark as Hell itself. A mushroom cloud rising into the atmosphere. The whole city leveled as terrifying waves ripple ferociously from the impact. Macht swears he hears the terrifying screams of agony from miles away. Does he feel accomplished now? Is his wretched soul finally at peace? No, never—this was only the beginning.

Okami is reaching his target. He can see it looming over the horizon—the majestic La Tour Eiffel. This is it: Paris, France. Okami releases his atomic bomb to detonate right above the Eiffel

Tower. The devastation could never have been imagined through words. We only pay its due in joining in the shock and awe at what has happened before us.

Around an hour before Hour Zero, Eddy is at a sports game, on American Eastern time, where the President will be speaking at half time. Along with him are two of his companions. The three are a secret team. Their duty today was to provide at-the-ready security for the President but from within the crowd. By half time, the smoggy European atmosphere will have exhaled its sorrow in time for American soil to receive the groans of the innocent souls lost to some unexplainable misfortune.

CHAPTER IV
POLLUTED WATERS

A change in perspective travels a great distance. Until further notice, the story will now be told from the original Eddy Malcolm's first-person point-of-view.

"Ladies and gentlemen, the President of the United States!" a voice said over a microphone. The President stalks up to the podium, with a stiff wave or two to the crowd.

"Thank you, a privilege to be here tonight," he started.

My stomach churns. The atmosphere is not right. Something is highly disturbing me. We need to get out of here, and fast.

"We exercise our liberties and enjoy the American spirit that comes alive with these events. We are competitors, but we are brothers and sisters," the President continues.

I turn to my left.

"Kathryn, we have to go," I whisper.

"What's the idea, Eddy? It's only halftime, and the President is speaking!"

"Something isn't right—it's time to leave," I pause.

"Hey, where did our third agent go?" asked Kathryn.

"She probably went to the concessions, look around," I insisted.

"Today, I consider this nation the greatest," the President resumed, "the global war is on the verge of its end! America will win! Our spirit is strong! Our people are loyal! We. Are. Free!"

Clapping and cheering turn into a harrowed stillness. A surreal feeling leaks its way into the air. The condensation of which drips onto the adrenaline of each person. Something's going to happen. When? WHEN?

"Kathryn, now!" I grab her hand and we rush down the bleachers.

"Where is she?! Rebekah!" I called out through the crowd of fans. We fight and shove our way through the sea. Each face is as puzzled as the next. Could a word be formed, it would fail to make a sound strong enough to shear the harrowing ambience. Then, it hit. The air raid sirens fade in and blare their anthem. These sirens signal an imminent air raid in the area.

"Shelter! Everyone, shelter!" said the voice over the loudspeaker. The stadium is adjacent to downtown. We just have to make our way into the one building with a bunker. That's all!

"This isn't good. Rebekah?" I asked once more. "Rebe- where have you been?!"

"I was hungry, I'm sorry! It seemed like a good time to-"

"Never mind that, let's go!" Kathryn, Rebekah, and I dash towards downtown. There it is--the intersection. And there is the brick building just past the street corner.

"Inside, inside!" I said.

"Wait, I forgot something!" said Rebekah.

"Rebekah, don't!" Kathryn and I said together. Kathryn cleared the entrance for us to climb into, brick after brick. We shoved the loose pieces back into the rubbled door.

"What are we going to do, Eddy? Rebekah's still out there!"

"Kathryn, she knows where to find us. We can't risk all three of us being caught!" Sounds of planes whir loudly above us, like a feeling of a living tornado coming. And it can smell your fear, and it is coming straight for you and only you.

"Eddy?" cried Kathryn.

"Yes?" I hushed my fierce tone to match her tenderness.

"I-I'm scared." She comes closer and holds my hand.

"I am too, but they will not find us. We are safe. Besides, nothing is scarier than I am," I assured. Up the broken staircase to the back wall we climbed. Once we reached the next platform, we knocked down the first flight of stairs before continuing. This should buy us time so we can hide. This floor is U-shaped. We are on the left side of it, and the space between is a room. The base of that 'U' is a hallway, with another room lining that side of the floor. We would hide inside the former room, in the larger space, as it is divided into two rooms.

However, before we turned the corner to get to the door, which faces the middle hallway, we heard voices. Two? No, three men. I do not know whose side they are on. We cannot risk a direct engagement. As far as they know, we are not here. Let's keep it like that. There is only one alternative I know that ends with our making it out alive; I do not wish to use it right now.

I feel around my waist to check for any weaponry. In my mind, I thought I had brought a simple pistol. Unfortunately, I had only a pocket knife and a folded paper in my pocket. I take it out and check the writing. I had forgotten Macht had slipped me a note before his departure. Why I am just now reading it must be by some divine intervention.

"Now is not the time to read, Eddy!" Kathryn scolded me. I agree, but my eyes cannot stop.

Macht wrote the following:

"The syringe of vengeance had its toxins injected deep within my veins. What a nasty side effect it gave me—a thirst only to be quenched by a daily dose of bloodshed. Only then could I be satisfied."

I am numb by this. He never showed these signs. How--how could I--? The paper drops from my grasp. In an attempt to pick it up, I made a rustling noise. Though subtle, it was just enough to catch the ear of whoever is on this floor with us.

"Who's there?!" one of them called out.

"Calm down. In this abandoned building, it was probably some of the ceiling hitting the floor," another said.

My heart rate quickens. Kathryn is right up against me, and I can feel her heartbeat too. It matches mine. I know we are both nervous. I have to be strong. I have to hurry. Something's up there. Do you hear it? Louder, louder! It's coming. Faster my heart thumps. I see their shadows. A quick judgment says their backs are turned to us. I seize this moment and take Kathryn into the room in the middle. There we could have the element of surprise. Here, I know there is an emergency weapon.

The papers, the papers! They are scattered. I can't find it! Hurry! It's getting closer! An empty silence. It is dark, I cannot see. I hear the door knob being grabbed. Oh, God help us! I can't breathe. You are my Shepherd, I shall not want. The haunting sound of the door hinges bombard the walls and back to my ears again. A single thud of a boot through the door. He turns his flashlight on.

"Who goes there?!" he said. The command shakes the room with its thundering bellow. As long as his light does not catch us, we are free. Stick to the walls, it'll create less noise, Eddy. I feel a teardrop on my arm. It fell from Kathryn's eye. I have to cover her mouth with my hand. I do not want to, but I have to so I can protect her. The grunt closes the door behind him so all he has is his flashlight to show his path. He steps on some papers and points his light at them. He finds himself stooping down to read through them. If he is in search of what I suspect, I cannot let him escape. This is my moment.

I bring myself to Kathryn's ear, and with a nearly inaudible volume I whisper at full command,

"Look away, and put your hands on your ears." I said. I have her face away as well. I sneak up behind the grunt and knock him out with a quick strike to the neck. I could not let the body hit the ground. However, I retained the flashlight. I do not change its position yet. The light is pointing toward the desk with emergency weaponry. I know my knife is in there. I make my way over and find a combat dagger in the top drawer. I take another look at the incapacitated body then back down to my hands, with the knife now in them.

What I am about to do--I fear--is something I will have to get very used to.

I look over at Kathryn, hands over ears and face still turned away. I approach the puppet-like body and with my hand over his mouth, I thrust the dagger through his chest. No witnesses, no worries. Goodnight. I lay him to rest once more.

I go back over to Kathryn and tell her not to look behind her because of the grotesque scene I have created. She puts her hands back to her side. There should be two more men out there. If I have ever felt the darkness of Hell, this is such a feeling in this room. I crack the door open slightly. I am able to get a visual of any action in the hallway.

The two men go inside the room across from us. I know there is a window there, and it is fragile. I run some numbers in my head for math that I didn't think I'd ever have to do. I need to plow into one of them while they are in front of the window to send him on a final flight.

However, the second floor is approximately only 15 feet above the ground. I do not want Kathryn involved, but I have no other option. I just remembered something pertinent. There are components in this room that I could use to make an improvised explosive device. I have Kathryn on lookout. I must act fast. For this to go over well, I need a way for it to stick. Tape! There is tape in the cabinet! And in another drawer I see... mounting tack! I will place the tape on the other side, so if he should grab it, it will remain stuck to his hand. By then, there will be no time left to remove it. I regret the evil that I have conceived; this disturbs me.

I move back over to Kathryn, who is still by the door, peeping through every now and then. Should mortal man delight in these heinous acts, he has lost all sense of his morality. For this were the fires of hell created, for this is what I deserve—that and one other reason. I have finished creating my sticky grenade. We take one more look outside into the hallway. They haven't left the other room, but they have left its door open.

I take the flashlight and chuck it into the far right side of the outside wall, opposite of the door. This way they think something is happening and one of them might check out the situation.

We wait for some response. Yes! Just as I had hoped, one of the grunts peeked his gun out and even fired a couple rounds.

"Come on out, I know you're here! Bloody chums! We're all friends. Come out," he aims his gun again slightly toward our door, "we're just your friendly neighborhood... OFFICERS!" He fired more rounds but we were opposite the line of fire. He has to reload.

"Don't be scared. We just want to know a few things..." I wait for his back to be turned. I have the combat knife ready, the stains of the last grunt still fresh. I see him reaching to reload his weapon. "...For starters, why were your planes in our skies?"

I must go. *Now*! I hinge the door open wide enough for me to slip through. Kathryn stands behind it but watches me.

I grab him with my arm around his mouth and slam his body into the wall. With a swift jolt I lance the knife through his back until he gives in. I let the body slide to the floor. I hear the third and final grunt:

"Stop all the ruckus, you'll get yourself killed, Harry!" No response. "Harry!?"

I motion to Kathryn, "Toss me the grenade!" (I would have to light it first anyway.) She is in horror and cannot move.

"Kathryn, if you don't do this, we'll both be dead!" She threw the grenade at me and slammed the door.

"What in blazes is going on out there?!" I take my position next to the door frame outside the other room. I have to strike right about...

"Harry, are you alright? You haven't answer—" He is an inch out of the frame.

I push my body into his and thrust the butt of his gun into his face. Before he can react, I slap on the sticky grenade and sprint with his body in front of mine into the window.

"Mate, what's going on?! What are you--" I ignite it. "What have you done?! No!!" He tries to grab it to throw it off but his hand is caught by the tape on that side. I force his body to break the window. I catch myself on the window frame before his descent. I count it down: 3. 2. 1.

"God strike you down, you cheeky—" *Kaboom.* It fiercely rattles the building and blows out part of the wall on the first floor. I do not like that. We have to evacuate, it is on the verge of collapsing on itself. It is far too old to stand another minute.

Kathryn and I will have to climb back do--we knocked out the second flight of stairs! I forgot! We'll have to risk a jump down to the first level. I ran back to the room to grab her. She is just sitting on the ground, bobbing in a fetal position. It is all too much for her, but we cannot make sense of things here, not now.

We still have no idea of Rebekah's whereabouts either. I pick Kathryn up and have her rest on my back.

"Eddy, I don't want to do this," sobbed Kathryn.

"Me either, but we have no choice. Something is miserably wrong. Those were British officers."

"What do you think it could be, Eddy?" she asked.

I have no earthly clue what to tell her.

"Whatever it is, we have another war on our hands is what it looks like." I said.

"But didn't we just finish the one that's been going on?" she asked.

Did we? If we dropped the bomb as planned, then didn't we? Oh... OH! The bombs! Oh, don't tell me... Don't tell me Macht dropped... Oh, God help us all!

"Kathryn, I fear that the bombs were not dropped where we had planned," I said.

"What do you mean?" she asked.

"My assistant was with me in the meeting. We discussed all the details there. He came out with a devilish smirk on his face. He even left right away after with people I have never met before. If he had something planned, then this is the start of the aftermath. I fear he dropped our bombs on our allies."

"Your assistant, Eddy? The private in the army? How could he have clearance? What smarts does he have to even operate the machines? Who is that man?" asked Kathryn.

"Kathryn, I have a confession," said Eddy.

"He's not just my assistant. He is my—" My words are abrupted by a chunk of ceiling falling down in front of us.

"Get us out of here, Eddy!"

"Working on it!" I rushed my steps. We come to the top of the stairs. We will have to jump to the platform.

"Are you able to jump for it?" I asked, with her still on my back. It can only be 7 feet across the way to the wall but 8 feet down.

"I can hardly even move. I don't think I can. I don't—" With what strength I have, I position her in my arms to get ready to toss her onto the platform.

"Eddy? What's going on?" She pleaded.

"Just trust me, darling." Thank goodness she is smaller than I. I launched her to the platform. She made it! My arm is actually hurting from that. Did I tear something in my shoulder? I feel a sharp pain there.

"Edward James Malcolm!! How dare you!!" She said.

"As if I had any other option, Miss 'I can't make a puddle-jump'!" I said from the second floor. My turn to leap. I land next to her and roll as I do, and she catches me by my side so I don't slip. I guess she doesn't hate me that much after all. I turn over to her as if to say, "Still need a ride?"

"I will carry myself, thank you." We get up and head to the bunker vault in the corner of the building on the first floor. We find Rebekah there. She has a briefcase in her hand.

"When did you—how did you?" We asked.

"Well, at first I wasn't sure because the usual door was sealed with bricks. But then this man fell out the second-story window and he sort of exploded and caused the wall to collapse. That's when I rushed to this bunker. This world's gone mad!" Rebekah exclaims. We can hear the rutters of planes whirring more loudly. Then a whistling sound. And another. And— Crash. Boom. Sounds of bombing loom around us up above. Our shelter quakes mildly, but it feels too close to danger. The ceiling lantern flickers as it whips around on its chain.

"Are those bombs?!" I said.

"Sure sounds like it!" Rebekah said.

"Who's doing the bombing?" Kathryn asked.

"Judging from our encounter a few minutes ago, I'd say British planes. Something is definitely not right." Kathryn's and my eyes open wide. We slowly turn our heads to look at each other. Our eyes lock. We had the same realization.

"The President!" We said in unison.

Our excitement was quickly met with an emotional drop. What would we even do? There's no call to action that we can answer with this situation going on. But that was the very reason we were here anyway—to protect the Chief. That leads me to another question: why did we run away to this building anyway? The one job we had—I could not do it. This is not good on multiple levels.

"Eddy, what do we do?" Kathryn remorsefully questioned. I thought for a moment. Really, what could we even do? We're sheltered inside this sealed bunker, there are bombers overhead, and at this point there are probably British scouts waiting to take us out from a mile away and without a trace.

"Kathryn, I think we should—" the conversation was broken by another bomb. This time on the building we're hiding under. Sounds of bricks collapsing roll into a thunderous, crackling cavalcade. Seconds, mere seconds, fulfill the story that anyone could interpret—the building has been decimated. The problem we face now is whether the bricks on top of the bunker have trapped us down here.

"You were saying, Eddy?" Rebekah joked.

"Never—nevermind." I retreated.

"Should we try opening the hatch?" She asked.

"No, not yet. In case they're waiting for someone to come out. We don't know if there's any more action going on." I answered.

"At any rate—Rebekah, what is in your briefcase?" My interest is piqued. Apparently it was important enough to risk her life over, I sure hope. She pulls her arms to her side, like someone that is hiding or protecting something private.

"Rebekah?" I asked once more.

Her stare drifts off, and her eyes become vacant. My shoulder feels cold. I don't like these feelings. Just what is going on?! I reach my hand to put on her arm. To my surprise, she doesn't withdraw. However, I don't move my arm yet. After a half minute, Rebekah hesitantly lays out her arms in front of her with the briefcase. Her mouth drops open, but her gaze is still empty. I remove my hand from her arm and look her in the eyes. A minute passed, and she finally spoke up.

"It's coming." She whispered. A teardrop trickles down her soft, innocent face.

"Rebekah, what's coming?" asked Kathryn.

"It's here." She points directly in front of her. Kathryn and I follow the direction. We see nothing.

Without a warning, Rebekah let out a blood-curdling scream.

CHAPTER V

AND THE WALLS CAME TUMBLING DOWN

Chirp. Chirp. Chirp. It's getting closer, louder, higher in pitch... But what?

"We are sitting ducks," popped up Rebekah hushedly. "Happy place, happy-"

"Rebekah, how do you mean? We don't know what you are trying to say." I said.

"What are-" said Kathryn.

"Shhh! Sh!" interrupted Rebekah. A whistling sound begins to whir up above us.

"Down!!" shouted Rebekah. An explosion blasted through the ceiling, knocking us all down. I feel the weight of rubbled concrete and rebar pouring over me.

My ears are ringing, and my vision is hazy and doubled. I try to mouth words but no sound comes out. I see two silhouettes through the gap in the rubble over me. It looks like they are trying to pick up Rebekah's and Kathryn's bodies.

I can't let this happen! C'mon, Eddy! I try to push whatever I can off me. I can see the two figures ascending a ladder. A third figure approaches me.

"There you are," it said to me. The ringing in my ear fades out, and my double vision starts to recover.

"What do you want from me?" I muster and cough. The figure ignored my question for now and grabbed me by the collar of my shirt through the gaps in the rubble. "

You're coming with us, criminal." he said. I am too weak to respond and black out.

I wake up in what I think is the back of one of their vans. No windows. We are on the move. I am leaning with my back against the side. A grunt sits on my left, and another across from me. Rebekah and Kathryn are not with me. My hands and feet are both tied with rope.

"Look who's awake," said the grunt across from me.

"Where are they?" I demanded.

"Don't you worry about them. I'd worry about yourself if I were you." replied the grunt.

"I said, where are they?!" again I cried.

"You don't seem to comprehend the situation that you are in, my friend. Maybe you're still traumatized, so let me break it down for you: we have the guns and firepower, and you are the tied-up hostage who's gonna keep quiet until we get to where we are going. Then, we'll think about letting you ask questions. Capisce?"

I grunted, sat back on the bench, and maliciously complied for now. But my mind does not cease to think about all of this. After a while, say, half an hour, the van came to a stop.

The grunt bangs the butt of his gun against the metal floor of the van a couple times.

"Why are we stopping? We have an itinerary to hold up!" No response.

"I said, why—" A sudden, loud thud came to the outside of the van's backdoor. The grunt across from me signals with his gun and a head nod to the grunt next to me to take a look through the sliding window and see what it was.

He shakes his head no, but it didn't seem like the commanding grunt was asking. He again motions for him to investigate, and this time he gets up to check the situation. As soon as the grunt slides open the viewer, he is knocked back as the entire door is knocked in.

The grunt across from me is shot dead before he can even react. I am feeling helpless and shaky, my heart pounding. The intruder steps up into the compromised van.

"Rebekah?!" I exclaimed with relief.

"Not quite." Rebekah presses a button on her wrist watch. Her entire body becomes a wavy, ripple effect, in a mosaic-like manner. Someone had used Rebekah's image as a camouflage. A person fully geared and complete with a futuristic-looking helmet appeared from the ripples. His coat is fur-lined around the collar.

"How is this technology possible?" I asked.

"You of all people should know, Eddy Malcolm," the person asked.

"Who are you and how do you know me?" I questioned.

"Tell me, how do you do it?" He started walking my way.

"I mean, with everything you've done so far, Eddy, I am thoroughly impressed you always seem to prosper at one thing: cheating. And let me be the first to say, I have been quite envious." A baffled look overcomes my brow.

"Until today." He reaches for a grenade-looking device on his tool belt. The letters "IRAG" are written on it. Without another word, he clicks it, pushes a button on it, and drops it to the ground, and leaves, his back turned to me.

"Who are you? What is this? Where are the others?!" I asked.

"Good luck, Eddy. You always seem to pull through. Oh, and he will be waiting for you." His voice trailed off. The grenade explodes with a bright flash of white light. I feel weird. My vision is turning black and it feels like I am going through a whirlpool. Wait. What is this feeling? Who- who am I?

"Hey!" I hear a female voice call out.

"Hey, Mister please, wake up!"

"HEY!! The news is on! Look! It's very important!" I am in a hospital bed, the television is on. The nurse gently nudges me awake even more.

"A week ago, we witnessed the most traumatizing events in our recent American history," the newscaster started.

A week? Have I been asleep this whole time?!

"And now, an update from our President: 'Thank you, thank you. Well, my fellow Americans, today we take some time out to reflect on the tragic events of last week, and how that is going to shape America going forward. Last week, on that beautiful Thursday, two American bomber planes that were meant to carry the atomic bombs to end the war with Japan were hijacked and used to drop those ungodly bombs on allied soil at London, England, and Paris, France. Words cannot describe how devastated we all are about this. We are aware of the rumors and gossip going around.

I am currently in the process of talking over it with officials from both countries, and we are going to find out who is responsible for this terrible accident. It has been reported that mercenary groups from these countries are trying to infiltrate our borders and take vengeance, but to them we say this: justice does not work that way, and we will find you too. We do not hide our American pride, so it is clear that imposters have wrought this evil upon the world. I can promise you this, that whoever is responsible for this offense will be swiftly brought to justice. Thank you, and God bless.'"

The nurse presses the power button on the television and turns it off. She walks back over to me and places her open palm on my cheek, tenderly caressing with her soft fingertips as she does, and works her way slowly to my chin. She then lets go.

"I can only imagine what it must have been like. We did a background check on you since you were out for so long, and your name is Edward Malcolm," she said.

The nurse cracks a half-smile.

"You have my total sympathy, Eddy, if you don't mind my calling you that. We all fail and make mistakes sometimes. No one could have predicted what would have happened that day. Please don't put all the blame on you."

I don't remember that day. It's not there. The memory is gone. I saw a flash of light and then... nothing.

"Darling, I appreciate it, but I haven't a clue what you're talking about." I said.

"I understand. You appear to have suffered a rather intense and traumatizing experience. We thought we lost you a couple times. You're a hero, you know? That's bold of you to risk your life like that." The nurse pauses.

"I know you will make a special woman very happy someday." She winks at me and proceeds to leave the room. Something starts playing in my mind against my own will.

"Eddy? Are you there? It's urgent." The voice sounds so real as if it's over the radio.

"I have to tell you something. I need you—" the voice crackles out for a second. "I need you to meet me at Zero Naught!" The voice becomes static. Why does that place sound so... familiar? Hm. So Eddy Malcolm, huh? That's a name I could roll with.

I wonder what he does, this Eddy Malcolm character of mine. I bet he lives the most adventurous and ambitious life to have this kind of praise or urgency wherever he goes.

I shall find out for myself.

The invading figure with the fur-lined coat, who is Okami himself, retrieved the grenade back to his own laboratory. Standing next to him was Macht. To their collective dismay, scans showed incomplete retention of the memories of interest. In other words, it was useless. The Malcolm Proper is still out there, along with his own mind still intact.

"Okami?" asked Macht.

"Yes, Macht?" replied Okami.

"It is apparent that we need to exercise different measures if we are to secure those memories for our glorious plan. What do you suggest?" asked Macht.

"We need to do more than just bring the battlefield to him. He needs to be physically placed on it somehow and thrown into the action. If we could get him strapped into a machine that replays his memories for us, we can record it and utilize that data as if the grenade worked the way we intended," suggested Okami.

"I have just the plan for that. You see, Eddy really likes numbers. Can't stay away from them. In his current state, he could be easily tantalized with irrefusable offers. However, we will need to wait a few years. First, he will be exploring who he is, due to the unintentional 'mind scrambling' error. Meanwhile, we can execute the perfect setup. When the time comes, he will become desperate enough because of his poor gambling habits. It's simple math. We will send out a personal letter of invitation to join our business. He will have no choice but to accept. After some mind-numbing there, he is as good as ours. He is a soldier after all; you just have to feed him the right orders like the dog he is. And, there's one more thing..." said Macht.

"We can reform the world?" asked Okami ambitiously.

"Precisely. It is on the cusp, you could say. It is struggling to stay on the tightrope, wavering with every government movement. We are like gods, Okami! We don't need government. But they definitely need us. What do you say?" asked Macht.

"I will return home with great honor and victory," replied Okami, who stood there pensively, almost tuning out what Macht was saying.

"This day has proven itself, as have we." Macht smiled. "I am thankful for the results. But now is the time to start the real work. Tomorrow is a new beginning."

A cold chill scurried down Okami's backside. Macht noticed this disturbance on his face.

"What is it?"

"I have this unnerving feeling. I cannot explain why. It feels almost like a heavy weight pressing against me. And it is reaching into the marrow of my bones."

"Well, it has been a long day. Perhaps you need rest," suggested Macht. "Perhaps you are right," said Okami.

No amount of rest will ever ease Okami, should he ever discover what he has truly done today.

Every action is irreversible, its consequences inevitable. When he uncovers the mystery of this bone-chilling weight, he will never rest again.

Okami, despite his accolades, was once a person of noble integrity. His egalitarian history, in tandem with his sinister machinations as of late, is catching up faster to him than he can visualize. To someone of his mental caliber, it is a deep affliction, a thorn in the flesh, if you will.

In 1894, there was born to us he who hails from a small Japanese village. That is, namely, Okami, the Wolf of the Axis. As a child, he delighted in being raised in his father's craft of steam engine design. Together with Mr. Walter Kysh, they pushed the limits on how such a machine should operate. They envisioned that one day the trains could be self-operating, one step short of sentient. However, the vision was short-lived once Walter went abruptly missing.

Heartbroken, Okami's father returned to Japan, bringing all sorts of unfinished schematics with him. Okami took the liberty of studying them and went on to the University of Tokyo in 1908 to study mechanical engineering.

His mother would regularly write to him to encourage him and send him small care packages. It was this love that kept him going. At the age of 18 in 1912, he finished University with highest honors and became an unparalleled force in his field. Okami revisited his father's notes and old schematics.

Albeit the idea of sentient machines was tongue-in-cheek at the time of conception, he thought more of that idea and wanted to bring it alive. He believed technology limited his father from achieving that goal.

However, the Great War saw other plans for Okami. He was soon drafted and was coerced to turn his noble passion into devilish weapons. It ripped Okami apart to see his greatest purpose being used as a militaristic agenda.

The feelings only worsened when someone broke into Okami's boarding quarters and attempted stealing his drawings. This is the moment that truly broke Okami. Those were his brain children. Outraged, he took matters into his own hands, eliminating anyone standing in his way. On the other side of the proverbial token, he believed he could never return home, being ashamed of what he had become and for what his parents would see in him now.

For his ferocity on and off the battlefield, hiding his identity behind a helmet and wearing his signature fur-lined bomber jacket, he was coined the name "Okami". By the time of the second World War, the Emperor of Japan himself delegated Okami to head the entire military. And it was working, until the day after Pearl Harbor.

Okami's highly respected friend and fellow engineer Jiro Horikoshi touched base with him on the matter, saying that this was an impossible war now for Japan. They eventually learned of the States' secretive plans and of this particular character known as "Edward Malcolm," through an intercepted letter, decoded by Okami, detailing plans for constructing a novel atomic bomb that would lay waste to Japan.

Not on Okami's fiery watch.

It wasn't soon after that he received word about an American soldier that escaped one of Germany's harshest and most fortified prisons. After tracking down this soldier, that is when he met Macht, and the future would forever be changed upon learning of Macht's plans for global unity.

In doing so, thought Okami, he could save his homeland as well as his passion. The perpetual course of the world would be forever changed. How peculiar that the outcome is anticipated to be the same, but the motivations and ideations to achieve it are incredibly different. Only time will tell when the vast calculus of it all shows these divergences.

There will be no heavier price for the apparent pursuit of death than the dissolution of freedom and life itself.

CHAPTER VI

THE TREE THAT BLOOMS UNDER FIRE

It is the year 1966. Eddy is in his 50s and has acquired an appreciably sustainable job at a prestigious accounting firm, after trying a few unsuccessful years at a factory nearby.

I stumble into work, that same old firm, bearing the weight of another uninspiring grind at the mundane. Perhaps it is better this way. Perhaps the world is better off with my cold, bitter hands toiling away at its profits. Would I have wanted it any other way, after all that I have been through? If only for a moment, that I could ponder it over, I would be euphoric. But the very next minute I'd be in absolute anguish for its bone-crushing gravity. Yes, this is the best way. I must be convinced of this, or I will spend the rest of my days fighting this battle in my mind. I could never win it; I was never able to do so. This curse—I would delight in shattering its chains. Oh, the devil it is. I would surely—

"Mr. Malcolm! How are you today, my good sir?" cheerfully said a coworker. I am honestly disturbed. Reality has hit me rather hard and unkindly in this manner. Did he just question my cooperative sanity at this ungodly hour? Take a deep breath, Malcolm. Let him have his pleasantry.

"Oh, why, erm, hello there! Fine, everything is fine." I glance around here and there, with a concentrated look on my face, I am sure. "Quite a wonderful day, I suppose. At this rate, I could retire from it before noon, eh?" I added for humor to lessen any suspicion on my mood. Normal people are fond of that, I hear.

"You're a funny one, Eddy! Bahaha, see you around!" The coworker goes on his way. Joy abundant. I couldn't have imagined a better way to spend my day than to 'see you around,' old goat. I am a terrible human being. Maybe this is the reason why I can no longer make friends, or was that on purpose? Who knows, and who would spend the time to do that math? I certainly would not. Useless frantic. Let me sip my life fuel in peace. My steaming cup of coffee is most assuredly a humbler companion.

I stagger through the hallways, a passing face here and there. I exchange a nod or two, per social convention. I feel imprisoned; the temperature of this cell matches the atmosphere of my being. Did I forge its bars? I'll find myself writing about that later, no doubt. What else shall I do? Human interaction is a resource I do not necessitate. Although, payday isn't a bad consequence of enduring those flames.

Moving on, the elevator doors open once more for me. Naturally, my shoulders are bumped back and forth by the rushing of younger coworkers against me. Who am I kidding? Everyone in this firm is younger than I.

Crowded, feelings of shrinking—but this is routine for us. I find myself in a back corner of the elevator. I overheard two ladies at the front.

"Did you hear?" Someone said. "The boss is trying a new program, and one of us will be selected to try it for free. He says it's going to help so many people! I'd like to try it."

"Quiet, quiet." The other responded. "I don't think we were supposed to know that. I heard it's using old nano-genetic engineering science tech-y stuff, or whatever they're calling it. Sounds kind of dangerous."

Nano-genetic engineering? No, I must be dreaming. Those are words I had wished to have never heard again. I got to get off this elevator; I want no part in overhearing this.

Good, this is my floor. I'll casually stroll to my cubicle and take it easy from here. It is going to be another normal business day.

"Ah, hello office." I say to myself. "Glad you're still in one piece and didn't burn down over the weekend or had too much to drink—or was that me? Heh. Alright, let's accomplish something great today!"

Two hours pass, about fifteen minutes before the first morning break. A lady's voice comes over the PA system.

"Edward Malcolm to the office, please. Eddy, to the office. Thank you!" Click. Oh, maybe they are finally going to let me retire. That would be bliss. At last, an escape, hand-over-fist! Every person in the hall inches his head out of his own cubicle to see me take the walk and bear witness, as if I am a prisoner on trial.

Perhaps, do they think I am the candidate for the boss's new program? I am only half-skeptical.

Knock, knock, knock.

"Come on in, Eddy! Wahahaha!" the boss's voice booms through the door. Grin and bear it a while, Eddy. This peasant has only one mindset: money. It's the only answer you need. You got this.

"Hello, Mr. Geld. Is there an issue?" I recite ever so spontaneously and professionally.

"Not at all, Mr. Malcolm! However, I do have a proposition for you." My skepticism is waning quite rapidly. "Hear me out, Eddy. We have selected you for our new program. Allow me to explain before you decline." He knows me too well. I do not like this.

"Eddy—" He pauses, his tone becoming more solemn now. Boss has never been like this before. "We know you were there, Eddy."

I take a moment and step back and stumble into the chair. I had no words to respond. Does he mean what I think he means?

"We know you were at Pearl Harbor. And D-Day. The memories are not all there, we know, but you were there. You saw everything. We need you to try our program. It can restore your memory. Your name will go down in history, Eddy! We will finally know the truth if you do this!

"Our two scientists are flawless in their works, and they're seeing results that have broken science! The nano-genetic engineering practice was revived and perfected just for this research. As far as they know, there are no errors or side-effects to it. What do you say, Eddy?"

Perfected? Those pretentious imbeciles know nothing of the science I fathered!

"I—I can't move," Eddy thinks to himself, "I know I was there. The memories are blocked, as if a barrier has been erected, and I can no longer visualize it all. There is something, I swear by this, that I have forgotten that was important. I need to know, but this will be my only shot."

"May I have a moment to consider?" Eddy said aloud.

"By all means," said the Boss. I stare down at the floor. It's my one comfort in this. Could I finally make the right decision? Yes! Wait—no, onward! Reckless abandonment! But what about...? Urgh, come on, Malcolm! What else do you have to lose by now?" I grasp the arms of the chair and stand up.

"Sir," I stood up quickly, "I accept."

"Wonderful to hear, Eddy! You start today. Right now, as a matter of fact." The boss presses a button on his telephone and it lights up red. *Bzzt!*

"Gentlemen, our client is ready!"

"Good," a male voice replied. I hear a door sliding open to my six-o'clock. It might've been hidden. I turned around, but there was no evidence for this sound. It must have closed just as soon. Two men stand side-by-side, wearing the most frugal and efficient-looking laboratory dress I have ever seen. I was relieved, in a way inexpressible, that I was not the one in such a uniform about to conduct some experiment. Those days are well behind me, and good riddance. I hope to never be reminded of them.

"Dr. Edward Malcolm, we presume?" said the taller man with black hair.

"That is correct," I returned.

"Do come with us. A pleasure, by the way." They guided me through the secret passageway and into a hallway. We are stacked single-file, I am in the middle. So far, only silence. This is most unsettling. A word, any word, might do me well. Forget it, I'll be the one to break the silence. A simple question will do.

"What is this program about?" I inquired. The scientist behind me answers, as the taller one guiding us has no interest in talking, at least to me. The scientist in front has black, wavy hair, which appears to be often neglected. I gathered this by its frayed-like array. I do not believe he cares in the slightest for constant hygiene. I will call this look the "insane octane".

"A mechanism by which we can retrieve and scan lost memories. Then, you shall be able to repossess them, only at a trivial cost. Think nothing of it for the service we provide."

"A cost? Some sort of deductible? Will insurance cover it?" I inquired half-seriously.

"You could surely state it like that. Yes, a deductible. How precise." If that wasn't an eerie answer, I just might be a white-collar clown of a different kind.

He and the other scientist start conversing in what sounds like German. I can only make out a word or two, but surely not enough to form a sentence. They speak it too fast. Their wits are on another level. I should be cautious. We approach the security door at the end of this hallway. The scientist in front of me inputs a complex code. I guessed it was complicated, by the number of beeps and clanks I was hearing per second. I estimated the frequency to be about 12. Not a single error. After 5 seconds of input, a chime plays, and the door opens. We step inside this new room. Lab equipment litters the walls, and a specimen chair, if you will, invites its participants to the north side of the room, or to my left from entry. The abrasive scientist hastes his way to a machine on the far east side of the room, and the other winds east-to-south around a row of monitors and stations to position himself.

"Eddy, if you would, sit in the chair. We'll be with you momentarily."

"Alright," I affirmed. I overheard the scientist at the south-side.

"Alpha-wave sequencing set to parameter N over Y interval, point-target transconductance aligned, setting neuronal gauge to..." He continued to mumble.

I secure myself in the chair. No bands or straps, I guess. However, above my head there is a dome-like structure just the right size for my cranium, if not slightly bigger. I am only somewhat nervous at this point. I've done experiments before on myself. Yeah, I can do this, no problem. I glance over to the madman at the east side. A grin has eagerly spread on his face. Whatever data he is inputting, it is causing him some ecstatic response. He looks up and over to me. I looked down out of natural tendencies. Maybe he thought something of my curious perusing. I shall let it go. The machines above me begin to make whirring noises, as the arms maneuver the dome barely above my head. No contact, all is spaced out. Not a single piece of equipment is touching me. What a peculiar procedure. Every sound ceases. I see the scientists exchange looks and nod.

"Is this going to hurt?" I asked the mad one.

"You won't feel anything you haven't felt before, old friend. As it were, you won't be able to know anything besides war. Just note that any decision you make, anything that happens, will affect this reality, and all others, too," answered he.

A brief pause intermingled with a confused look from me followed. A sense of familiarity crawled its merry way down my spine and sent impending doom on its way back up.

"Okami," the madman called out.

"Yes, Macht?" asked Okami.

"Do it," said Macht.

My eyes spring open.

THOSE NAMES?! HOW!?

NO, GET ME OUT OF HERE!

DEAR GOD, SPARE YOUR MERCY!

"Okami?! Macht?! No, you're—"

Sssssssssttt.

The machine growls and hisses, lights intensify.

Darkness, I see darkness. No, I see bright white.

"Like I said: I can't wait to see you, Eddy," Macht ridiculed with a mischievous, bellowing laugh.

CHAPTER VII

A COLD WITNESS

This reality fades. I am entering—seeing—some dimension? I hear a voice, it is calling me. It sounds like Macht's, but the tone has changed with a lowered pitch.

By some confounding mechanism, I am eerily able to observe myself in this dimension. There is no one else around. I can only see the bright white light as before.

"Who are you?" I demanded, breathing heavily.

"I am your conscience. You formed me into this sentient entity, so you wouldn't feel lonely."

"Hm. So I did," I responded. The white light was gone now, and there sat a few feet in front of me, facing me, someone waving together his forefinger and middle finger of his right hand, darting back and forth from the outside of one of my eyes to the other. My eyes were locked to this hypnotic motion.

"Recall to this program what you know. We know you know. You do not need to hide it anymore," said the Voice.

He stopped his waving motion. Almost inexplicably, I was able to focus. He has the letters "EMDR" stamped into his forehead. Is this a Shrink of a different caliber? Whatever the case, it appears to be working. I couldn't hold it in anymore, the tears drained by themselves like a dam that had burst. I didn't want to, but I had to. It is shearing me apart to remember what I had experienced. I've never before felt a sting this painful or this cruel.

"...After that, we never saw Rebekah. Or, at least, for a very long time. Town after town, we fought. One regiment at last shut us down. We could only live if I let her go to them, which would inevitably split us apart, probably forever. Last thing I saw was a garage door closing. They transported me to virtually nowhere, but the truck was ambushed. I was the only survivor. I became a hostage, but I was spared. Rather, I was a trophy being passed around, but I'll take it. Their masks looked peculiarly tribal. They wouldn't communicate with me. We just sat in silence. They gave me a pen with a journal, and I knew somehow just what to do.

"I drew them a symbol everyone should hate. They got wired up and exchanged looks with each other. My next move really grabbed their attention. I put an 'X' right over the symbol and ripped the page right out. I crumbled it and threw it across the table. I let them know what I thought. They were very pleased to say the least, but they had me cross my arms and rhythmically tap like that for a solid minute before the next step.

"I was not sure what else to expect, but I will tell you this: Pearl Harbor changed us."

My voice uproars and becomes aggressive, as a drill sergeant to his platoon.

"We were ready. We simply weren't putting up with it anymore. A tragedy like that, on our turf, our soil? I don't think so. Give me a break; we'll show you a real firefight!"

I collect myself once more. I see the Voice in front of me gently and slowly jot some notes.

"We prepared the nastiest weapon any of us will ever see. Our scientists called it the atomic bomb. It was a beauty, but, at the same time, a devil.

Were we ready for this kind of warfare? We questioned our morals, but that didn't really bother us at the time. We were more concerned with ending something on a bigger-picture scale.

"We turned the war around quick-like. But the enemy wouldn't surrender. That's when we decided that it was time. Against our best interests, we gritted our teeth and prepared our planes. Something else didn't feel quite right that day. I couldn't put my finger on it, but something just chilled me to the bone. My hunch was right. Our planes were somehow being piloted by men that weren't ours. The courses were originally set for Japanese cities. Hiroshima first, followed by Nagasaki. The plan was to go one-by-one, then eventually Tokyo.

"There was a problem. Two planes and two bombs took off that day. We couldn't stop them because we had no idea. "We never would've guessed where their actual destinations were. London and Paris. At the same time. With American planes.

"Do you think we could've ever negotiated our way out of that, with how diplomacy was at the time? It would've taken more than just a miracle. It would take a whole other revolution."

"What do you remember about Pearl Harbor, Eddy?" asked the Voice.

"I was just outside the base when I saw it happen. Every second was another whistle through the atmosphere followed by a haunting bang that would take with it another soldier, another building, another battleship. It could never take away our will to fight.

"I see before me lay the decimated forest of ships. I am standing, alone. I call out for any survivors. No replies. I suspect no other survivors here. Through the thick smoke, I can see the silhouette of a man coming out of the hellfire. It's approaching me, closer and closer. I can't move. I am too weak to fight, but I want an answer. I see his full-face helmet and notice the bizarre markings. His bombardier jacket has similar symbols. I have heard of the rumored 'Wolf of the Axis,' but is this him—the one they call 'Okami'?

"He comes before me and eyes me up and down, followed by a deep sigh of apathy and vexation. 'Doctor Edward Malcolm,' he begins in an ominous tone. 'How fortunate of you.' My hands tremble. How does he know my name? Two more men emerge from the smoke. They are carrying someone by the arms and dragging his legs against the unforgiving ground. *It's Sergeant James, my brother-in-arms*! When they reached us, they punched the man in the face and blindfolded him. 'James!!' I screamed, horrified and addled. 'So you know this man,' said the Wolf.

"Okami pulls out his revolver and cocks it. I see an engraving on the barrel: LT-8. Without another word, he sends a bullet through James' temples and tosses the corpse at my feet like its a ragdoll. 'Hm. You know, he originally survived this. But don't worry, Doctor Malcolm. You two will meet again in hell, I'm sure.' He turns his back to me and walks off with his two men.

"I dropped to my knees... The scene before me is nothing but scorched earth. This grandeur-turned-desolation of a battlefield will never be forgotten. Pearl Harbor, I will remember you. You will be avenged! This is not the end for us! We will fight! We will win!"

"Ending transmission. Thank you, Eddy," said the Voice. No response.

The signal waned as did this reality.

CHAPTER VIII

ZERO NAUGHT

Reality as I know it fades back in, and I find myself sitting on the edge of a bed of a bottom bunk in what feels like a bunker. I grab the journal and pen next to me on my right and record my sentiment, should these be my final moments:

"My name is Edward 'Eddy' James Malcolm, and these are the years of The Resistance. These United States have become a foreign territory yet again. I describe my struggle and efforts to reunite the country and eliminate its foes.

"This melting pot was never meant to be boiling over with the heat of deception and conflict. Allies? Enemies? There are only people that are not you, and you simply cannot trust them. That man who was your caring neighbor and helped you when you had an emergency? You now have to end his life the next time you meet; he just might have to do the same to you. How can you both be sure you can be on good terms if you allow the other to live?"

My writing is disrupted.

"Private Edward Malcolm, front and center!" Someone uproared. I peer up from my journal—it's the sergeant. He dons his silver helmet which also has a visor. His full-sleeve army-green jacket menaces his figure that much more.

I see the name "Sgt. James" embossed into the upper-right corner of the jacket.

"Get up! We've got a war to fight!" He roll-calls again to me. It's always another war, the world will never be satisfied until all of its hills are graveyards. I put the journal and pen down and strap on my boots. I finish preparing my uniform in all its glorious tatters. It has been used by soldiers before me; it was all that could be found. My toolbelt barely straps together from how worn it is.

"Get your weapon, Malcolm! The clock ticks!" He ordered. As I do, I look around the bunker. All the beds are empty. Am I alone? What is the rush?

"Where is everyone?" I questioned.

"Either six feet under or dead on the field, much like you are going to be here if you don't hurry! I'm leaving with or without you, Private!" He stated. I should know better than to ask stupid questions. I search the weapons crate for my gun. It's been labeled with the name "LT-8" on the grip. I've never used this model, but it is a 9-mil no doubt.

There's an ammo box next to this crate. I scavenged some rounds and two magazines. No primary arms could be found. This is what I get for snoozing in.

"Up the stairs, Malcolm! You first! I got your six!" He directed. The pathway is cluttered with boots, empty rounds, plucked-out shrapnel pieces, and some stains of blood on the stone floor. How much action did I miss? After some struggle, I managed to get to the stairs. There is a hatch that must be opened to continue climbing.

"You'll need this, Private." He handed me a steel pulverizing ram, small enough for both hands to wield it by the handles. I take position, left foot forward on a step and right foot anchored back.

And as I step upward with my right foot I pound the door with the ram next to the locked handle. Whoever designed this method of security needs a lesson in engineering. There is a much better way to use a door. I unlock and open the hatch and continue through it.

"Done, sarge!" I said, still looking forward.

"Good job, Malcolm. Now," he pauses, "you die at last!" I looked back and his revolver was aimed for my head. His face looked almost like Macht's now. Without a second more, I launched the ram at him, from my right hand pushing on the back side, in the direction of the gun. His bullet ricocheted off during its flight.

The ram knocked him off the flight of steps and to his death onto the crimson-painted stone ground. I went down to search his body. The look of Macht was no longer found on his face.

Further searching yielded this ID card with a black strip running across the lower third of the back. I confiscated the card and tucked it away in my pocket. I wasn't sure what to feel, but I kept going anyway.

The stairs end at this platform, and another flight continues to my left, parallel to this one. At the end of that flight of stairs, I come to this small hallway, and I can see it wrap around to my left. The flooring is dark oak wood. On the opposite side is a door, centered in that wall. I approach the door. A closer look shows a red button, which I assume should open this door. I pressed it, but nothing happened. There is zero chance of my breaking down this latched metal door with my foot. A witness would be amused, but the effect is fruitless.

I notice wires running down from the button. It leads to a mainframe on the wall a couple meters away. I see a sort of translucent panel built into it, and the panel contained a small rectangular protrusion with a hollowed space in the middle. Inspection tells me there is a magnet behind the panel so as to be able to read something based on a polarity interaction.

I remembered the ID card in my pocket and took it out to see if the panel would read it. After a few swiping attempts, the panel made a buzzing "click" sound.

It worked! A red diode on the button by the door lit up. I should be able to open the door now. I put away the ID card and walk over and press the red button. The latch retracts into the wall and the door turns inward about a few inches. Lights in this new room flicker and sequentially actuate—I see this through the ample crack of the door.

Once inside, I immediately guessed the current purpose of this room: storage. Beneath that superficial aspect, it became clear it's a library—a highly disordered labyrinth of a library that shows absolutely no resemblance to a library. Nevertheless, it is a library of sorts. Boxes, crates, and lockers look as if they were tossed into random places. To my right, there is a computer-like system huddled in a niche. To my left is a terminal that I guess has some connection to the system. I try to boot up the computer system. By some miracle it turns on. The miracle turned to quick disappointment.

The system asked for some input code to allow access. //Access Restricted. Code required.

//Awaiting input. . .

[ ]-[ ]-[ ]—[ ]-[ ]-[ ]

Six digits, huh? How hard can this be? In this forest of manuals and dispersed materials, I am guaranteed to find the access code. Whether I have to deduce it or find it point-blank, it is in here.

Papers here and some there—like leaves in the fall—decorate the floor. I glance, I scan, I move on. I find a crate with two numbers carved in it: 4, 5. Alright, noted.

Around the room I prowl, looking for the slightest hints. A bucket on the shelf has the numbers "1" and "9" knived into it. Okay, that's four numbers—two left. More scrutiny—depths to which I go, I know not—have I passed what I needed? Perhaps, is my mind now numb to what I am desiring? I can feel a burning sensation in my eyes and an ache in my forehead. I wonder how many minutes ago I lost my ability to reason. I need a fresh stance.

Somewhere in this littered jungle there must be some reprieve. Aha! Gotcha! I lounge on a dilapidated, black-and-white chair. I do not care for the integrity of it, I'll be up long before it— Crunch! Nevermind.... On the ground I sit, no less than by destiny itself slapping me upside the back of my head and knocking me down to this humble position. My eyes wander aimlessly, mostly from my eagerness dissipating.

A portrait, there on the wall! The face in it—I can see the final two numbers engraved. On either side of the face, I faintly notice "2" and "2". That gives me 5, 4, 1, 9, 2, and 2.

In what order? Well, this could take either some sound logic or random gibberish. I'm not the best at solving puzzles, but I like making them and watching others suffer, so basically I'm an engineer. The first shall be last, so I shall put "1" last. Then a "2" most follow behind it, quite naturally. It could be, by coincidence, that "9" was added from 4 and 5, so those must be the first numbers in the sequence, how else could you get 9 later?

And that leaves the other '2' to come after those first two.

That gives me 4-5-2-9-2-1? Yes? Yes. Let's try it. I hobble up from my sitting position and drag myself to the terminal. Once more, the interface appears and asks for the code. I input the sequence, and it spits this out:

//Access Granted.

//Press Return Key for more options . . .

It gave me a few options, which read from top to bottom the following listing:

"History of the World, 1939-194?"

"Read Transcripts"

"Mortality Database"

I decided to start with "History of the World." A question mark in place of a year for the decade we are currently in does not add up. Did history suddenly stop? A one-page document entitled "What We Know" appeared on the screen.

It reads:

"As of late 1945, world history has taken a turn for dramatic change in the course of events ever witnessed. This one-page document is the only written information available on the history of anything since the beginning of time. The victors of the Second World War had every history book known to mankind burned. Any historical recording that wasn't a census was to be, and we quote, 'disintegrated or otherwise disposed of such as to not have a physical existence.' By their policy, this page is not legal to exist. Reading this page will endanger your life. Every two sentences, someone new has had to come along and add to it, because the previous writer was murdered mid-way. Approximately 55 lives have been martyred to this cause and just to finish this paragraph. "I found a way to conceal this document.

"If your name is Edward Malcolm, you need to add to the page under 'PH-HI-43'; there are instructions there for you. You will not find that page on this machine, however. You must go out and find it; I cannot tell you where, my life depends on it. Actually, change of plans—I am using my last breath to type this, Eddy. They know. GO!"

*** End of Recall ***

A newly found responsibility has been weighted to my shoulders, wrapped around my chest, and tied down to my belt. I shut off the machine and leave this room. Not sure what to think—I need to go. Somewhere. Not here. It doesn't feel right. Nothing feels right. Reality? Fantasy? Neither? Don't think about it, Eddy. Just go! Facing outside the room, to my right is another hallway. To my left was the staircase to go back down to the bunker.

I travel down the hallway on my right. It's a straight shot to this open room, four walls. A door is on the opposite side from me and centered on that wall. A 360-view of this room before I leave shows me there is not much here of further interest. Science posters, calendars, cork boards with notes—it's not much to me. I go through the door. This room is rather large.

First, it fans out like an isosceles trapezoid, then horizontally splits off either direction into what I assume are hallways. After those gaps, it continues straight on for a while until an adjacent wall connects them to make the exit. I would guess a football field could almost fit in this room. I can see a downward dip half-way across, like a horizon, and can hear water flowing from that direction, but I do not see any. Before I move, to my left is a computer station and two vending machines. A faint neon white-light overhead guides me to the oasis. To my right, if I were to draw a straight line from the station to the other side, I find lockers and storage crates and shelving units. Not much excitement there, or could there be? I might investigate, I'm feeling a little curious. I know my mission is outside that door, but if I never come back here, it would be a waste to not have indulged one last time.

I go to my right first. I feel a strong pull that I cannot resist or explain. I walk past the shelves and jumbled freights and think nothing of them at this moment. I see the door where this hallway ends. The knob is golden, curved—elegantly inviting—with an extravagantly designed pattern. Its door, easily told, boasts a mahogany-type wood. The finish has been polished until you can see a faded reflection.

Looking down, I notice the concrete flooring transition into a brass divider that separates it from burgundy carpet running into the room beyond this door. I take a deep breath, clasp the door knob, and close my eyes. I can feel happiness in my being once more.

I am ready! I want so much more! I CAN BE SO MUCH MORE THAN THIS!

I turn the knob, burst through the door and open my eyes to unprecedented freedom. This sight is everything I dreamt my heaven could be. I lust after paradise; I am deprivation incarnate. Feed my starving soul, that I may live once more. Dearest beloved, I plead with your spirit—love me the way I am meant to be, satisfy our longings. Do not think a moment more, do not hold back on our destiny—we were meant for each other.

No.

No? You do not think so?

Never.

Where are you going?

Wherever.

My love?

Who?

No! Come back! What have I done? I can forgive—I will go to any length to keep you! *I'm sure you would, that must be why I'm leaving.*

My dear? Please?

The door slams shut by an irreconcilable force. Before me now is my greatest aspiration: the casino.

This room is dedicated to a great time. The middle of it is the bar, with a rectangular table outlining it, naturally.

In a corner is the roulette table, a billiards table, and some classic slot machines. All this—hailed under the perfect lighting: light enough to see, dark enough to cheat. Of course, no one would admit that last part. It's part of the game! But, then again, no one makes bets like I do.

With great risks comes even greater tricks.

There is a small problem with this paradise. I am the only one here, as usual. This grandeur—it runs its business on my making a fool of others, but without others it is putrid waste.

My darling was right (I should've said that long ago): I didn't give up my other love. I couldn't equally love them both; I always poured more and more of my efforts into my gambling. And this time, I finally lost. And I lost everything. All of it—gone. I thought I had it all, I thought my life was together. It is clear to me now I have lost. And she's not coming back. Could I ever find her once more? By chance, if time would allow it, I could.

How inviting this scene is, but how lonely I am. I want it no longer. I seek a new longing.

I left my 'paradise.' I closed its door softly, my head hanging down. I turned my back to it with the palms of my hands having slight contact with the door. Nothing more—I say, nothing more to gain, nor a thing more to lose.

Straight ahead, I see the door at the end of the other hallway. Since I've already wasted so much time, I might as well be trivial a while more. I sense some nostalgia about its qualities. I go over to it. The casino door makes a mockery of this one's fashion.

This door is typical oak, very matte with a bright finish, whorled randomly, tucked tightly in the darker rivers coursing through it. A small rectangular window pane, vertical in its placement, is nested at just below eye level, and extending almost to the top. It has that thin black diamond-like pattern weaved into its frame.

Peering through the window, I can see yet another stretch of hallway. On either side of it, I can guess that rooms must diverge here and there. I reach down for the silver round door knob and push my way through.

Every step sinks me to the ground. It brings childhood flashbacks. I swear it's the same haunting memories just like the old days.

Bitter! Cold bitterness—ever lingering, ever pungent. It strikes me to the core, lancing each deployed barrier on its way. I thought I reinforced them?! Burn in the hottest Hades, never come back to me! No! It is not! I did my best! Shield your eyes before I gouge them out. What was that? Never you mind, spawn of the abyss! Fight me to the death, I shall not lose! I am braced in the armament of honor, and I bolster the code of sacrifice as my weapons of warfare. I gain whether I live or die, but your death will only be loss.

Edward! What are you doing? Do you feel anger? Hatred? Is it unquenchable? Your blood is boiling over. You have that look in your eyes. Focus! Come back! Don't let it take you! You're better than this, Malcolm! I slap my face with a stiff left-hand sweep. *AGH!* There. That should be good enough to alarm my senses to pull me back into reality. Well, that is, a more real dream than that nightmare. The first classroom is on my left a few feet away. I have a pounding migraine. These few feet feel like a mile. How crippling, how imprisoning.

The classroom is empty. That's all anything is anymore, why do I even bother expecting others to show up? Someone left writing on the chalkboard. I maneuver between the desks to get a better glance.

The phrase is in what appears to be German, with a French caption below it. The phrase reads something along the lines of "The Wolf swims in vanity, but the Hawk crosses the river dry." The caption must've been added later by another, I guessed from its different style of handwriting. From what I can glean from it, it says, "Run. Fast."

How inspiring. I wonder what the hurry is.

Suddenly, I hear the sound of guns cocking behind me. This should be good. I raise my arms above my head and turn around.

There are two people with heavy weapons aimed at me. Their combat stance suggests they aren't messing around. They step aside to let a third person, unarmed, come through. When he appears in front of them, he stops and eyes me like a wanted prisoner.

"You, fellow. Name, rank, alignment?" He asked me.

"Eddy Malcolm. Private. None," I replied.

"Guns down," he ordered.

In synchrony, the two soldiers retract their footing, square up, and move their guns to the sides, barrels pointing up.

"Could you be the long-awaited Edward Malcolm?" He questioned.

"I am who you ask for, but for what am I long-awaited?" I said.

"Rumor has it you have connections to storm the so-called Fourth Reich, to stop Macht, and to end this War of all Wars. As your father before you, you have the engineering knowledge to give us the advantage. Come with me, and we can help you make that happen."

I have untold skepticism about this. I'm no genius, but in my current state I cannot do anything but yield. I slowly walk over. Halfway there to him. An uneasy feeling. Gunfire hails from behind and drops his guards. He turns his back; I take advantage of that and pull the dagger from my toolbelt to his neck.

A smoke bomb was thrown and filled most of the room and thinned out away from its source at the doorway. A squad emerges through the fog of war, all wearing some kind of gas mask. Four. No, five of them, I counted. I can sometimes count. This is one of those times. I hear them yell out in some language, like a blend of Russian with French (I wonder how that came about?). I look forward to this.

One of the guards was crawling away, but one of the super soldiers dragged him back into the smoke and finished the deal. I would normally have a mortifying terror right now. That is, if I had any emotions left. I think my right eyebrow raised and maybe my left eye twitched a couple times, if that counts for something.

This one super soldier is wearing some type of helmet with a glass visor that extends from the nose to almost the middle of the top of the head. He approaches me while the others secure the room. Again, more eyeing of my person.

"Malcolm," a deep, low-pitched voice said. It sounds like the voice is filtered through the helmet to hide an identity.

"Hello there," I said, unsure of what to say anymore. It's my last resort before sarcasm, which I know will get me killed. My hostage is petrified at this point.

"Give him over," he demanded.

"As you wish." I retract the dagger and release my grip on him. The soldier took him by the arm, glared intensely for a mere second, then pushed him into the other comrades. He had the same fate as his guards but more swift.

"Am I allowed to ask questions?" I said. If the vizer weren't on, I swear I could tell I was just given the most irritated look. I'll take that as a resounding "no." I notice there is a left shoulder patch with the numbers "317" woven into it. The other shoulder has a patch with the name "Lt. Nyrthak." What is the significance of the number?

"I have something to show you," the ominous soldier said. They lead me outside this branch of the building and to the main large room where the exit is. We go across the staircase which bridges the upper and lower floors. I was right, there were waterfalls on either side of the staircase, flowing gracefully and gently.

"Malcolm, this door is only meant to be open under one of three circumstances: the resistance has failed, the resistance has won, or Macht is dead. When I open it, I'll let you take a guess under which condition I am doing so."

The soldier inputs a series of codes and undoes a number of locks. Finally, he turns a wheel as if to roll a vault door open. Clanking can be heard by the two massive steel doors prying apart. Sunlight beams from the outside through the space just created and gradually spreads out as the doors do. We creep outside, exchanging looks, for this is a rare opportunity. I am blinded by the bright light.

"Malcolm, what do you see?" The soldier asked. My eyes adjust. I see...

"Devastation, wreckage, apocalyptic horror, and unspeakable catastrophe," I said.

"Who won?" asked the soldier solemnly.

"I... The resistance... has lost?"

"No one won, Malcolm!" The soldier threw an arm back and planted his feet.

"But this war's not over. You decide that for yourself. My time is up. I will see you later, assuming you choose the right path this time, Eddy." The super soldier and his squadron press a button on their wrists, causing their beings to fragment like shattered glass and dissipate into nothingness in the atmosphere.

I had too many questions to be left alone like this. I turn this way and that. All around me, aside from the building I just exited, are only marks and scars of destruction. Dilapidated buildings whose bricks are trying to hold together at all costs are scattered throughout. Where am I? What God-forsaken world is this?! What happened here?

I face the building I just exited and glance upward at it. Above the doors there looms an engraved sign that reads plainly:

Zero Naught

...

...

Is this...

home?

CHAPTER IX

ARDENT PROFIT

I traveled down whatever road remained, and ended up in a ruined city after a few miles. I was greeted with what I believed to be a black-and-white sign that some would presume to be for welcoming; however, I could only make out two words: "Market District." Below that there is a line that was obviously painted in later, declaring the phrase "Home of the 0116."

This concrete jungle has had a few of its trees chopped down. Of what lay before me and of what is to come, I fear that which is inevitable: the cruel winds of change. As I wander further into this rotting municipality, as all are, I see a small crowd of 7 members standing in a circle in the street. There is obviously no danger of traffic. I feel an instinctive urge to join in on that. They are too occupied to notice my intruding.

"What's going on?! My signals are all scrambled!" One of the women cried. Judging by her highly decorative gear, she must be the leader.

99

"The city's been ravaged. What do you expect? Macht will stop at nothing until he gets what he wants. It's how it's always been!" Another woman said.

"My squad has been at it around the clock trying to find a solution. There's got to be a way to end this madness!" a hooded figure chimed in. "

We're trying our best over here!" said the first woman. "There's only so much we can do. The ratiocinator specialist has to keep a low profile these days because of what he discovered about Macht."

"A whole town is dead, and no one finds this in the least bit suspicious? Let's think twice about our priorities now..." the hooded figure said.

"What's the point? With 'kill-on-sight' active, no one knows if inspecting the casualties is worth the hassle," said the second woman.

"We could find what each of the deceased had in common. That's a start, don't you think?" replied the hooded figure.

"A risky start," commented the second woman. The hooded figure noticed me. His eyebrows raised and his gaze sneered.

"I see a risky start right in front of me. Our fearless 'leader' has come back to redeem us, haven't you, Eddy?" he said. They all turn to look at me.

"Oh, pray tell!" He continued.

"What shall we do, Eddy? Is this not what you wanted? Well, here it is! We hope you're satisfied!"

"Calm down a second, will you! Eddy did not intend for this to happen! We all know that!" The first woman said, defending me.

"What is the meaning of this?" I asked.

"Haven't you heard?" answered the second woman.

"Macht is bringing one final plan together that will ensure his reign. He's going from town to town making sure of one of two things: either no survivors, or no free thinkers. He calls it a 'beautiful balance of subjugation and submission'."

"Then we'll have to stop this regime," I rebuked.

"So simple! Why didn't I think of that? Oh wait, because it is near impossible!" scoffed the hooded figure.

"That means it's still possible, no?" I threw back at him.

"Why don't we regroup at HQ to discuss this?" the second woman suggested.

"I like that plan better," agreed the first.

"Wonderful, I'm looking forward to it," delighted the hooded figure.

"Great! Except, you're not coming with us," replied the first woman again. She steps out into the middle of the circle and faces him.

"What do you mean?" He questioned with a puzzled look. He drudges a step back and puts his arms forward.

"No witnesses." She fired a round into him. The crowd left behind the corpse to rot. The leader takes my hand—I show no resistance. There would be no point, and I feel as if I am on their side anyway. An odd date, but I'm okay with it. Dinner would've been nice. She looks familiar, but I do not entirely recognize the face. They take me to their headquarters.

We are in this simple room with a decent-sized briefing table in the center with typical ceiling lamp lighting directly overhead. Naturally, it is dark. One door to enter, one door to exit. The leader steps out to grab something. The remaining six of us just stand around the table.

What do we discuss? They do not seem too worried about that. I guess words are long lost these days. She comes back with a rather large rolled-up parchment in her hands and a toolbox with what grip she has left. She lays the parchment across the table. It's a map of the district. A folder loosely-bound with string was hidden in the middle. It looks familiar somehow. Who knows what all is in there. She was too enthusiastic to care, she swept it off the table onto the ground. She used both hands to get the toolbox onto the table. It makes a loud clunk and slam from the contents inside--presumably metal instruments. I am not volunteering for any surgery that these witch doctors want to perform, even if they had a license for that kind of practice.

We watch carefully. Not a word is exchanged just yet, we are growing antsy from anticipation. What is she going to do? What's up her sleeve? What can we expect?

She pounds the table with her fist. We all jolt.

"First order of business, my 0116!" She yelled. She opens the toolbox and dumps all of the contents onto the map. A lot of them are rusted over. There's a geometric compass, a geographic compass, a protractor, screwdriver, a few wrenches, some dice, wooden figures, and a hodge-podge of random junk. It must be sentimental treasures to her, I'm sure. No sane mind would still keep all of that. She spreads out the items with no particular purpose yet so she can get an overview of her inventory.

"We don't have much time. In fact, we may not even finish this meeting. Let's be quick and real." Her gaze switches between each of us so she knows she has our attention. I love this woman already. She's just my type.

"We need funding, commerce, supplies. Here's the problem: there is only one outlet for us to do that. The ratiocinator will be our primary directive in figuring out the costs, in addition to another task only he and I know about. Under no conditions is anyone allowed to know that task. Do not ask, you will just be shot without warning." Everyone sort of freezes. This satisfied her. Should I tell her she has placed her left hand on my right hand? I think I just lost whatever focus I had.

"Moving on, I suspect that—" she stops. Her eyes slowly roll as if to detect some sound.

"You're kidding me! I just got started. They're here. Positions!" She flips the table forward to use it as a guard, the contents on top pouring all over creation. Apparently the table has armored plating on its underside, and the two legs on her side, I see now, had some mechanism that let her easily manipulate it. She is a tactical genius, no doubt. The others take some formation that fans them out. I hide behind the table with the leader and the ratiocinator.

Everyone pulls out his own gun. All sounds of prepping stop. Echoes of footsteps travel around the corner and into our room. A grenade is tossed right at the table but it bounces back into the hallway. You can hear from someone out there a very loud foreign phrase which I assumed was a harsh expletive, judging by his reaction. It was a concussive grenade. This room was built to withstand the reverberation of those sounds and absorb any outside light before it reached three feet past the doorway.

"Who designed this ungodly fortress?" I whisper-laugh to the leader. She has a grin from the amusing attempt of the invaders.

"You did, Captain Malcolm." She answered. Captain?! How long have I been fighting? What achievements have I accomplished? Who has given me this title, and under what ranking system?

"Captain, you and the ratiocinator specialist have to get out of here. Now!" A look around the room shows no other means of escape.

"Where? How?" I asked.

"To our three o'clock, slide the bookcase to the right, pull the telephone mount down, and raise up the picture frame. Type in this code: 0116. Got it, Eddy?" She instructed.

"We have your back, go!"

"Affirmative," I said. I take the ratiocinator with me, and we stay low as we stealth across the room. I follow her commands and enter the code into the hidden keypad.

Mechanisms cling, sounds ding, and cogs turn. A trapdoor appears to exit to somewhere more secure, we hope. The small hallway is black. I take a final look back.

"Take this! Eat some lead!" They cried. The door closes. We hear only gunfire now. The hallway lights turn on, probably from some relay. There is an elevator shaft at the end of the hall, we can see. We make our way over. It's a caged type of elevator the size of a phone booth. There's a single red button. I press it. The door opens to the elevator, making haunting sounds between its rusty hinges and the tunnel-like reverb of the hallway.

We take a quick look at each other. There was no other option but to hitch a ride, so we sauntered inside the iron coffin. The forsaken metallic doors close rapidly this time. Clank. The ratiocinator pulls the lever on the floor of the elevator. Up we go! At the top, the doors open but there is a wall where the way to exit should be.

"So I don't know how else to say this, but with all due respect, your title is kind of a mouthful. Got a name, Mr. Ratiocinator Specialist?" I asked.

"Name's Marshall, I'm responsible for calculating the odds of winning at any given moment...Mmh, among other things. One thing at a time, Cap'n."

"Right. How appropriate," I agreed. Marshall sets up a device on the wall, turns a few knobs, flips a few switches, and steps back. He has some trigger in his hand. Upon depressing it, the wall is no longer there, as it exploded from what I guess was an impromptu mine he had planted.

Clever. However, our hopes are quickly shut down as a group of strange thugs rushed over to take the ratiocinator hostage. We had no time to react.

"Look who it is, on a silver platter!"

"Don't worry about me, I'll be fine! Just go, Eddy! Save yourself! Hey, guv's, watch your hands, filthy scoundrels!" cried Marshall. They try to turn on me but I manage to fend them off with my pistol. I retreated back to the elevator. They took an axe and severed the cord. I fell roughly 15-20 feet before the old rusty thing was unable to move. They didn't bother to check on me.

I'm not sure what they plan on doing with Marshall, but I have no feasible way back up there, and I cannot go back the way I came. I pry apart the top bars of the cage and manage to worm through the crevice I created, miraculously unscathed. Given the distance from one side of the elevator shaft to the other, I see no reason why I shouldn't be able to shimmy my way back to the door.

I create an equilibrium with my body against both sides. Surely enough, I grudgingly inched my way back up. Falling is not an option; I'd rather die to the thugs, it'd be much cleaner.

At last, after 15 painful feet I get to the point where I can grasp the ledge of where the opening was made. I peek first. The room was deserted that quickly? Or did Marshall give them a piece of his mind? I curl my body, make the most of my core, and hustle inside into the room. I give myself two options: exit through the window or use the stairs, which I suppose could lead to using a window at a lower floor to be safer.

My instincts at this point tell me to go down a floor and attempt an escape by a window. The architecture is unique enough that I can essentially either climb down unharmed or jump to some adjacent rooftop and to the ground. Let's try that, Eddy. I heard there was a sort of sanctuary in this town, I have to get to it. They say I'll know it when I see it. Something about a certain symbol on the front door and the pattern repeated around the building.

I open the door to the staircase, my body, of course, being behind the door so that I am not taken by surprise. Nothing. Not a sound, a shadow--no sign of life anywhere. Where could they be? How? Nothing is adding up. At this rate, I should've just jumped out the window on the floor above me and let destiny have its pitiful course. Ah, pull yourself together, Edward. I'm hungry, that sanctuary better have edible foods, nothing like the stuff I had back at the underground bunker. My taste buds would have more ecstasy from expired hardtack. Guaranteed! Not that they'd be able to tell at that point what food was anymore, but the point still stands in my mind's eye. Is being delusional a side effect of absolute madness? I'm more than guilty at this point—as charged, governor. I successfully evacuated this building.

Across the street is the sanctuary, I can see its speckled banners wave gallantly. The heraldry is music to my eyes. If I don't get an ounce of rest, I just might have to change my name so I don't get associated with being someone smart like Eddy Malcolm.

Look at me, I have a Ph.D. in nano-genetic engineering! HA! What a joke, what a clown. Get your act together, the circus is long gone. I spent the next few days here in this sanctuary. Yes, I did find substantial rations to recover my senses. The residents here are extraordinary and rather finely-tuned peoples. This is pure glory, it is.

After a while, a messenger runs in to find me. He has this scroll-looking newspaper. A rather primitive method, but the timeline as it stands is too broken for me to care at the moment. The message, it reads, is an urgent call for me to go to the hospital to see someone. There is no name given, but they will know where to take me when I tell them, apparently. I shall make my way over as soon as I can.

I am at the hospital now. Waiting, just waiting. That's all life is anymore. How much longer do I have to wait to live again? The nurse comes out from the door. With her clipboard in hand, she calls my name forward. This feels like a judgment day. I do not know who is waiting to see me. Frankly, I am terrified. She leads the way. We turn the corner and walk down this hallway. It seems to never end with each step we take. To my left and right are doors every so often. Some are open.

The scenes I—the sounds, the smells—witnessed were too grotesque for me to pen; that would mean I would have to mentally recall the horrors and then regurgitate those visuals in such a way for the reader to empathize vividly the said horrors. I would rather not impose that on any other person. God eternally forbid.

We take a sudden stop. The nurse never did give me the name of the person I am visiting....

"Mr. Malcolm, this is the room." She says gently and sorrowfully, as one would in paying his respects.

Of what could she be remorseful? Should I be ready for some disaster? I start to reach for the door knob. My hand is frozen. My hairs are on end; my heart rate is increasing more and more. I just might throw up if it beats any faster. What is this? Why can I not move?

"Are you going to be okay, Eddy?" She asked. She puts her left hand on my right shoulder and lightly rubs it.

"I—I think so." I am losing my balance. My vision is hazy. I am definitely sweating right now. My voice—it's gone. I hug the wall, I have a feeling of falling over. It's blazing hot in here. Is it just me? I'm parched. My side slides down slowly against the wall.

"Eddy?" Her face is a blur to me. Another nurse sees us and brings us some water. Meanwhile, the first nurse is attending to me still.

"Here, Eddy." She gives me a cup of water. It's cold. Refreshing. Reality comes back to me. I rise back up. The nurse has both her arms on my shoulders.

I see the face of my lover on hers. It's been a while since I've had the arms of a caring person on me.

"Are you feeling better, Mr. Malcolm? Looked like some heat exhaustion. I know you're nervous. We're here for you." She opens the door for me and heads on in. I cautiously step inside. The thud of my steps pounds my eardrums. I keep my gaze fixed to the ground.

"Eddy, if you don't look up you're going to run into me." the nurse said to lighten the mood. When I do look up, I see the nurse's face. To my left periphery, I see the bed. The figure in it is in a blind spot. Do I dare look?

"Eddy? Is that you?" The invalid figure called out. The voice was hoarse like one with a respiratory infection. It sounded like it took almost her whole strength to say it. I have to look. I don't want to. I tilt up my head and lift my gaze through my fedora. If I could clear my throat of its chokehold, it would again be constricted by what I saw.

It's Rebekah!!!

"Hey—" the greeting was broken by another lung-hacking cough. Her smile pierced me. I bawled. Such beauty, even in life's ugliest moment.

"Closer, c-come closer, Eddy," she beckoned me. Why can't I talk? Why can't I find words? Speak! SPEAK!! Nothing. *You coward!!*

I pace myself to her bedside. She so gently takes hold of my arm and works her way down to my hands. Her grip is so weak. As she strokes down, her face lights up and she starts to cry. Her perfect smile just shines so gorgeously.

"You're so strong." she commented. She looks back up to my face, somewhat hidden by my hat. She nods for me to remove it. I do so.

"You're looking more like a man, Eddy." she added. I look over to her heart-rate monitor. It's slowing down. The nurse comes over to take her blood pressure. Sixty over 60.

"Y-you're dying, Rebekah?" *Why were those my only words so far?*

The smile fades. I took away her last joy. What kind of man even am I? Pathetic. I was supposed to be there for her. Darn you, Eddy!

"Mmh." Her heart rate is slowing.

"I'm not ready to go. There's so much I've wanted to do, to see. I-I'm not—I'm—"

"Rebekah, take it easy." She motions to punch me but her arm doesn't make it.

"At least," she said, "I had the privilege of loving you, Eddy." The smile returns. What do I say?! Tell her!!

With her final breath she says to me,

"Goodbye, my love."

The heart-rate flattens. Life has left her. But death wasn't strong enough to take away her smile. I was the last thing she saw. Her gentle hands leave mine. I delicately set them on her stomach, one clasped over the other. I step back from the deathbed.

Who am I?

"Call it, nurse." One said to the other. She checks the wall clock then her own watch.

"One sixteen in the afternoon," the nurse called.

I check my watch: Three seventeen, it reads. What is going on? The hands spin backwards, counter-clockwise, faster and faster. Feelings of dizziness slam my senses. My eyes are dimming. Knees are caving in. I hear the nurses trying to say something but it's too faint to my ears. I try to grab onto something but it's no use. I collapse. Darkness again, just like when I entered that one dimension. The darkness becomes bright white light. Is this going to be another one of those experiences?

"Eddy..." That familiar tone cries out. I find no consciousness to respond.

"Eddy, what was this?" I don't understand the question.

"Did this actually happen, Eddy? Was it your own memory or a fantasy?" The tone demands.

If that was fantasy, I never want to dream again.

"Well, Eddy?" it asked again. I responded with the answer I wanted to believe:

"Fantasy."

CHAPTER X
WINTER'S DECEPTION

I find myself back at the sanctuary. The sobering experience of what has passed has numbed me head-to-toe. Where do I go from here? She's gone.... She's gone. I repeat to myself over and over. I do not believe it, nonetheless. She must still be alive, I tell myself. I'll bring her back, whatever it takes. I won't accept this defeat. No, not this one. Not this one!

"Mr. Malcolm?" followed by a knock at my chamber doors. Who has invaded my chambers?

"Is Edward Malcolm here?" again preceding some stranger audibly testing the durability of the wooden doors. This person better have a good reason for pestering me. A rush of bitterly cold air sweeps over me. I look over to the windows. There is a hole in one of them—as if a stone were violently chucked at it. I can see that it is snowing as well. I pull my blankets up closer to my face. A closer inspection of my person reveals that I am very naked? My clothes lay off to the side.

A charred stick is next to the pile. Perhaps—somehow—in a delusional state of mind, I removed them to start a fire to relieve my coldness. Excellent logic, Malcolm. Just excellent. I use my blankets as cover while I put my clothes back on.

"Ahem, Mr. Malcolm?! I. Am. Waiting!" The male voice called another time with solemn irritation.

"Come in, do come in!" There was no other option by now. He flings the doors wide open and barges in like he runs this cathedral. He is wearing a tophat and a suit and wields a tapering cane with a golden sphere at the other end. His mustache is to be commended for its fitting nature to the wearer: strict, slightly swirly, mildly uncomfortable, and definitely incongruent in every aspect of the word.

"Edward, hello, good si—Good heavens, my boy! Have you no shame?!" He blunted. He adjusted his monocle. I was still struggling to re-clothe myself.

"Hmph. I have brought with me to share with you this fine message from the King of Enterprise himself. It's an offer you can't refuse, good sir!" He pulls out a ribbon-wrapped scroll from his coat. "Go on, take a look!"

I finished getting dressed and tossed the blankets aside.

The message read the following:

"To our brother Captain Edward Malcolm: If you are still out there, we need your help. The front line is being absolutely decimated. IRAGs are tearing our men apart. We're being pinned down to our last resorts. Macht's forces are driving us out. Rendezvous point — Ironshark, LT-8, coordinates: 25-67-33. Be here, stat!" — Lt. Nyrthak, Resistance Division 317

I slammed the scroll to the ground and grabbed the man by his collar.

"Answer me now, and I'll let you live. Tell me—is she alive?"

"Of course, Edward! Settle down now!" The man reaches his arm behind him. "This is the sanctuary! We wouldn't want to get blood on these grounds, would we?" I released my grip and took a step back.

He retracts his right arm and violently swings it forward with a knife he had hidden on his belt. I stop him by grabbing the side of his wrist with my left hand.

"No, we wouldn't." I thrust my right fist into his gut. He drops the knife and lets out a hard grunt. I confiscate it, walk away, grab my satchel, and head toward the exit.

"You listen here, Malcolm." He said as he coughed and caught his breath. I stop but don't turn around. "You will die— Macht will win."

I step outside the sanctuary. His voice is getting louder.

"Don't you walk away from me!" I felt my ankle being grabbed. I kick back as I turn around. It struck his jaw.

"Malcolm! You are guilty and you know it! Judgment will have its way!" I stoop down and take the knife out from my satchel. I motion to stab him, but he flinches and closes his eyes. I scoff.

"So you still have fear? Hmph. That's a good feeling."

"Why don't you just kill me like the thousands before? Huh?" His breathing expedited.

"Because I'm not my counterpart. You still have a brain you can use. Let me know when you decide to use it." A puzzled look flooded his face. I continue to walk away, trotting through the thin layer of snow.

Church bells ring, the haunting sound fading into nothing with every forward step of mine. I have with me my light-weight steel armor underneath my clothes, a basic iron helmet in my right hand, and my trusty leather satchel wrapping around my right shoulder and chest so that it rests comfortably on my left hip.

The road outside the city extended for roughly a couple miles. Off to the side, eventually, was a supply shack. I raid it for what it's lesser known for—vehicles. Particularly, the shack had presumably broken-down motorcycles left-over from the War. The one I chose—the dull green one—had a slight problem of its own: upon inspection, the brakes were nonfunctional. There are no tools to fix this problem. I fill the tank anyway with whatever fuel is left in storage. I must be committed to whatever direction I go, being mindful of my speed.

I scavenge the shack for non-perishable foodstuffs to fill my satchel. I take off with one goal in mind: I will see her. Down some turns, around some bends—the trees on either side of me are my only company for an hour or so. Some of the trees, for a seemingly unexplainable reason, were black-and-white.

Finally, in the distance I can see buildings. Whether this is my stop, I cannot tell. The snow is blinding. This town's entrance has a wall looking about 30 to 40 feet high, but I do not see any guards. I kill the gas to my vehicle and stop the motorcycle roughly a football-field out and listen for any sound. It is as quiet as a church mouse crawling across carpet. I feel nothing but the chilling breeze of this glacial winter across the flaps of my jacket.

Wait—I see a figure running towards me. I can see he has a heavy scoped rifle in his hand. I figured if he wanted me dead, he could have done it when I was a mile back.

The closer he approaches, the more I notice he is wearing that same type of armor I saw back at Zero Naught—charcoal black, a highlight of color on a single shoulder, and an armband to match that color.

Perhaps there's a ranking system related to the color?

"Soldier! Sign?!" He said. I do not understand. He pauses in his steps. "SIGN!!"

He raised his rifle.

"Ironshark!" I exclaimed back, unsure what to reply. It must have been the magic word, because he lowered his gun after the fact. He starts to run to me again and stops about ten feet from me.

"Why are you here? Do you not know this is a highly restricted area?" He asked.

"What area isn't restricted these days? I'm here to see an old friend."

"Does this friend have a name?" The interrogation thickened.

"You could say she goes by Lieutenant Nyrthak. My name is Eddy."

"So it's you. Say no more. Come with me." I leave my motorcycle on its kickstand by the side of the road and walk back to the gate with him.

Am I expected to trust this grunt for the whole journey? What if I am led to some back alley and gunned down?

In front of the metal gate, we stop. It stands at a height of what looks like 30 feet. He taps the ground twice with the butt of his gun. The gate starts to rattle, splits at the middle, and gradually retracts into the side walls. The moment we step inside, the gate closes again and its mechanisms lock it tight. We mount a vehicle down the street. A one-horse open sleigh of a different kind is what this is. He and a driver take us to the town square, which is a tad off-center from the middle of town. A few soldiers of similar uniform are bustling about, chatting away. One of them peers in our direction after we have stopped and parked.

"Corporal Adams! Front and center, soldier," called the presumed commanding officer.

"Lieutenant Nyrthak, I have brought to you a man who claims to be a fellow by the name of 'Edward Malcolm'," replied Adams.

Nyrthak is wearing a helmet similar to the soldier that last talked to me at Zero Naught, right before disappearing. Nyrthak sizes me up and eyes me down.

"So you have, have you? I'll be the judge of that." Nyrthak comes up to me, rifle to the side. This officer is wearing enough gear to spare four recruits at least.

"Tell me, 'Edward Malcolm,' what is it that you want with our camp?" asked Nyrthak.

"I desire nothing, but if you are able to spare it, I could use some rations and a resupply," I answered. Nyrthak chuckles mockingly. The other soldiers join the chorus. Nyrthak stops, and so do the others.

"Did you hear that, comrades? This guy wants us to send him on his merry way, complete with bed and breakfast! Stop that, you'll actually might make me have a happy feeling for once!" I am becoming rather unsettled as this progresses.

"Do you have any idea who I am, you peasant?" Nyrthak asked, in a rising tone of scolding merriment. He grabs me by the collar.

"Actually no, now that you mention it. I did quite literally just meet all of you, so...." I responded sarcastically, against my better judgment.

"Ugh, you sound like Eddy, that's for sure." Nyrthak released and pushed me, as if I had no contribution to her amusement. I dust myself off and fix my collar, the soldiers again chuckling at me. The bell-tower sounds off. Four bars played. It is the top of the hour. But which hour?

"Well, would you look at that? It's your lucky day, 'Eddy'. High noon. You're coming with us to 'La Ville Folle'," said Nyrthak.

"T-to the what?" I asked.

"Crazy Town. You're living in it, son," replied Nyrthak smirkingly. We all hop in our vehicles and drive off to this old "Wild West"-looking shack.

Inside, Nyrthak invites me to this round, wooden table where it is just the two of us. She takes out this rolled up paper and unfolds it out onto the table. It has all kinds of black ink markings on it. Is this parchment paper from an ancient era, or something? It looks as if it could spontaneously disintegrate if I coughed hard enough in its direction.

"Now that it's just us, you can stop with the games, Eddy." Nyrthak quietly said.

"What do you mean? Do I know you from somewhere else?" I asked.

Nyrthak took off her helmet, and whispered to me with a grin,

"It's me! Kathryn! But don't tell a soul I told you, or else!" She put her helmet back on.

"Kathryn?!" I whisper-shouted. "Is it-is it really you??"

"Yes, Eddy. I wish we could have a proper reunion, but we have something to discuss. Don't mind the ambiance of this make-shift tavern. I had to get the boys distracted somehow, God rest their weary souls. Who knows the last time we had a true Happy Hour around here."

"Kathryn, tell me what happened, or what's happening. Was that you back at Zero Naught?" I said.

"I formed this resistance shortly after the stadium incident. And indeed it was me, but it also wasn't. It's complicated. I find it best not to understand, but rather to accept what was. It helps with the coping. These people you see here? All commonfolk. I found them on the streets and gave them a home and a second chance."

"Coping, what? Ok, besides all that, what were you trying to say with all that?"

"Think deep. Your memory chip, Eddy! We can reassemble it, and restore your memories of this world, so we can take down Macht! Look!" She points to the drawings on the paper. It has three separate shapes forming a square.

"In order to successfully assemble it, our scientists say you first need to visit three distinct places of your life in which they would be found originally, if that makes sense."

"Umm, in a round-about sort of way, yeah. You could say that."

"Think, Eddy, what were the three places you spent the most time? The factory, because you spent time researching machines; the office, since that was your job for a while; and here, downtown. You don't remember, but you've been here before many times helping us with campaigns."

"How do these all correlate, Kathryn? What's the purpose, the goal? What is the exact connection?"

"The brain fog is getting rough on you, isn't it? You should read up on your own life's history. We need you to have your memory chip, so we can find the Baron Rogue and stop Macht's plan of assimilating everyone through his IRAG grenades. From what the ratiocinator has told us, we think he's using those weapons to become immortalized, and if that happens... Well, it won't. Urgh! Don't you remember when he dropped those bombs on Paris and London, and blamed it on the Baron Rogue? This is our chance to take back what's ours!"

"I will do it. Okay, I know you just mentioned it, but where do I go again? This is a lot to process all at once, Kat."

"That ol' factory you worked at, remember? There was a side project you left behind that needs to be attended to. In your old notes I saw that you mentioned a sentient steam engine machine. I think now is as good a time as ever to finish it, don't you think?"

"What kind of project?" I asked her.

"You mentioned something about drilling through the walls of corruption. We could certainly use that, whatever that means. And something else about a giant robot with a grenade launcher, which thoroughly excites me. You have to go there for sure now."

"And of the office?" I asked.

"You always talked about how toxic of an environment it was, how it drove you mad little by little, until you finally exploded one day and left without a trace."

"How soon do I depart for this mission?"

"Tomorrow might be nice. Take today to prepare. We'll keep in touch, don't worry. No more separations or disseminations, got it?" She insisted.

"Understood, Lieutenant!" I said.

"Good." She slides over a small, string-wrapped parcel. I give her a look of bewilderment and proceed to open the gift. "It's part one of your memory chip. You're welcome." She removes her gloves and shows me her somewhat mutilated and scathed hands.

"Thank you, Kathryn. I have many questions, but thank you," I said, still in shock. She slips her gloves back on her hands.

"Come with me, I have to show you something." We leave our table and step outside the door. I had a sudden burning question for her.

"Kathryn, wait! What about Rebekah? Where was she all this time?"

"That is a name you do not speak! And the 0116 are a perfectly capable group under her leadership. No more questions!" answered Kathryn.

A figure awaited us outside. He's adorned with a fully-encased looking-glass helmet and a coat whose collar is lined with fur like that of a wolf.

"Kathryn? Is this what you wanted me to see?" I whispered.

"N-no, Eddy. It isn't." Kathryn moves her hand to her side gun slowly, finger to the trigger.

"Hello, Eddy. We need to talk," said the figure. Kathryn pulls her gun and shoots at the figure. The bullet goes straight through, for the figure was only a projected image.

"What level of sorcery are you playing at?" She demanded.

"There is no sorcery here, only science. I am the one they call 'Okami'. I show up when things don't feel right. And everything you two have said tonight does not feel right at all, I gotta say," said Okami.

"What do you want from us, Okami?" I asked.

"What I want is something only you can give, Eddy: your life, on a silver platter, to our doorstep. That is what I want! You have one week to show up, or we'll find you ourselves. We already control your minds, just surrender the rest of your pitiful selves. Got it? Okami over and out." The optical illusion vanishes in a converging, spiraling motion.

"Eddy?" asked Kathryn concerningly.

"Kathryn, I—what are we going to do?" I questioned, still worked up, involuntary trembling. An unsettling pressure invades my sinuses.

"We're going to assemble your memory chip and defeat them. That's what we're going to do, that is why you were brought here. We've come too far. It is time to strike back against this endless oppression. Finally, we are one. You have the piece I gave you. That leaves the factory and your old office. There's a room for you here if you wish to stay until morning. Time ticks away, Eddy. It's your call what to do with it." Kathryn walks away.

I decided to book a night here until the next morning. Tomorrow, everything changes. Tomorrow, I will fight. But today? Today I will rest and recuperate.

I fell asleep and dozed into a dream. Around me now are the walls of honor. Two strong guards march my chained-up person down the aisle of judgment. The crowd eyes me down intently with every step. Each step increases the weight of the chain. At the end of the aisle, it becomes too heavy for me to walk.

"Have a seat, Malcolm!" the guard thrusted me into my seat on the right side of the split. On the scratched-up desk was a rectangular label stand that read "Defendant."

Am I on trial? What for? I look to my left and see Macht and Okami as the presumed plaintiffs.

One of the guards yells out,

"All rise for the Honorable Macht!"

At once, all knees did obey, except for mine which could not move. The guards had chained me to the desk and chair. The judge thundered his footsteps down the aisle of righteousness. Louder and closer were they announced. The steps stop next to me.

"Hmph. It seems our defendant has no respect for the law." The steps marched on dignifiedly. Judge Macht takes his seat on the throne of jurisprudence.

"Order. Plaintiff, state your case." Macht stands up.

"Your honor, we find, in this court martial Edward Malcolm to be guilty of 317 different war crimes, on the account of dereliction of duty, civil inordinance, negligence, abandonment, and an abysmal amount of infractions and misdemeanors!"

"Thank you, have a seat. How does the defendant plead?"

"Not guilty, your honor," I said. The entire jury gasped, the courtroom quiet for the span of 3 seconds, ensued by hushed mumblings.

"Order in the court! Dr. Edward Malcolm, I presume, are you even aware of the accusations against you, and is this truly how you plead?"

"Your honor," Macht interjected, "perhaps we should settle this formally and democratically."

"The defendant has left me no choice, after all. Bring it out!" The two guards brought out a roulette table and some dice.

"I heard you love to gamble, Eddy. This should be only a moment. Let it ride!" declared Judge Macht.

"The Honorable, Magnificent, Omniscient Judge Macht is letting it ride!" A guard clasps the dice in his hands, blows in them, and tosses them into the spinning table.

"What?! You can't do this! Your Honor, where's the evidence?!" The judge ignored the question. He was all too excited to gamble.

"Who all bet against Eddy today?!" asked the judge. Every hand in the jury shot up like a spring flower. They started jumping everywhere, shaking each other, and roaring like madmen in a cage match. It was comparable to rioting monkeys at a zoo. What difference did it make? As it is above, so it is also below. That is to say: like father, like son. The dice ceased in their reckless, prejudiced dance. As the dice toppled to a complete stop, the jury died down and faded away from reality. Judge Macht expanded to ten times his size and grabbed my shackled self by my shirt.

"I will make you fear me, because you just will, and there is nothing you will do about it, as the past has already shown. You are guilty, because you did do this," said Macht firmly. The judge-like attire dissolved as Macht's brilliant royal armor replaced it.

"But I won't send you to die, because I'm not my counterpart." Macht shoved me away then snapped his fingers on his left hand.

I woke up, the chains and courtroom gone.

The dim reddish-orange light of morning pierced through the window.

CHAPTER XI

ILLUSIONARY MALAISE

Morning. A time of fresh renewal. It always brings such a pleasant sense of undertaking.

Until today.

I will decide for the betterment of myself and this world. The evil I have wrought, I had let consume me. May my name be forged in iron among the fallen. I went to report to Kathryn, but no one knew of her morning whereabouts. It's time to depart.

I set out to make my way to the factory's campus. Along the way I stopped by a dilapidated town.

I see a group of children playing, about 16 in number. They are divided 8 and 8 on either side of a snow-laden trench. It appears as if they dug it themselves, judging by the rough design. In synchrony almost, the children all dipped down to gather a bunch of snow to form a snowball. Some of them had wooden sticks resembling guns in their hands.

About 3 seconds later, either side violently threw their snowballs toward the other. I was taken aback while also somewhat amused. But the amusement faded upon realization of the attempted violence. Once their round of frozen artillery ended, I presumed, I approached the giggling anklebiters quite cautiously. I asked them about the meaning of this sport they are playing.

They replied, "It's called 'kill on sight'! We see someone and try to kill them! The adults are all playing it, too, but they are lucky and have real guns and weapons. It's super fun, you should try it! Hehehe!" they giggled away and went back to playing their twisted game.

I continued on my journey, unsure what to think or make of this.

There it is. The factory of once-upon-a-time. This old place stands upon the feeble foundations of those who have ridiculed timeless work in order to gain far less than they actually intended. I scoff at them. Their life's work is now in ruins.

If I could ever decide upon a remark, it would be rather prejudiced. How is it that a soul can wake up every day and consider himself so confident in his arrogant ways, yet in reality it is all fading and rather quickly? Surely, poverty struck them faster than they could render a reason. And as such, through spending more than the company's earnings, it came to pass. The inevitable.

I am here for one reason, and solely that said reason: I want my memory restored, and this place holds one of the components to doing so. I believe strongly that it is my only defense against Macht.

In this time of trial, I have to explore as much as I can to accomplish this, if I wish to truly save that which I have lost and may very well lose. I cannot be complacent or apathetic. My downfall will find me faster than I can find myself, and it already is. I have tread these grounds once upon a time; I can tread once more. I will not enjoy it, no, but the least I can do is face it head on.

I pause a moment in my thoughts. An uneasy feeling has entered across the doorstep of my being. I don't want to do this. My breathing. It's rapid. I feel lost. Where am I going? Where is this place? Have I been here before? EDDY! Snap out of it, just this once!

I brace through it once more, but my legs feel like jelly. You know what? They will hold me up. We've been through this before.

Once more, just once. MORE!

I timidly put my hand upon that rusty, worn-down, grime-and-gunk door. Its oxidized and dystopian colors definitely show just how disgusting the hands that have touched this door have been. Materialistic, savage, repugnant mongrels, that's who. The evil that's been wrought, I must relive the memories no matter how evil.

Finally, I push through the door. I find myself in a lobby, with wings on either flank. I urge myself to the left, where I discover a door on my right. There is a label engraved into this door. Perhaps it was someone's former office?

The plate reads:

"The grave of someone who left behind their most prized possessions in this room."

I oscillate in my thoughts to even consider why a factory office would be someone's grave, but it does make sense, and I know that which I seek is in this building somewhere. I fumble with the doorknob and bravely open the door. "Oh blimey, what is that horrid smell?!" I exclaimed to myself as I am bombarded with the uncomely stench of putrefaction, presumably.

There is a bed in here that appears to haven't been made since the dawn of time, and there are papers scattered all over the floorboards.

As I gaze clockwise around the room, starting at my nine-o-clock, I see a staircase, a computer terminal, shelves with surplus, a roulette table, and a desk with a journal on it to my four-o-clock. I head for the terminal first. Upon boot-up, I am greeted with this lovely invitation: //Please enter Password to continue. Lovely indeed.

Per usual, my gut instinct was to consult the journal for any sort of clue or warning sign telling me to abandon all hope or what-have-you, so I can finally approximate my senses. The journal was already open to a bookmarked page.

The page reads:

"Dearest beloved, I have failed you. I commend your strength and effort. Let this testimony harmonize with you: Do not become as I am. Get out there, and change the world. Do know this: ZZC-85B-TDE. Go!"

I scramble back to the terminal, dodging all pieces of trash littered everywhere as I do. I wouldn't dare dream of a better day than cleaning all this junk off my shoes. Alright, I'm back to this electronic hunk of metal. I may or may not have knocked over a century-old bottle of who-knows-what on my way back over. I input the code I found into the computer. The screen reads as follow:

Welcome. Initializing setup
"Access again for your options."
I press the return key. The next screen starts.
//How may I help you?
Three options are available:
"What is this place?"
"What happened here?"

And

"Solve the puzzle to obtain the Key."
Let's go right down the line. I chose the first option to start.
Recalling data...

The computer screen blinks and refreshes. "These are the memories of the man who died here. Everything you see was his treasures in life. The things he held onto the most."
Onward I scrolled.

** Recalling data… **

"A man was murdered in this factory years ago. Identity unknown. It is now run by some militia, per last year's protocol. Extreme caution is advised."
I will try the computer at its own game to obtain that key.

"What is the value of the following sequence,
in which 0 = +1, and 1 = +2?"

"0-1-1-0-1," it printed.

I am confident in my basic arithmetic skills. But just this once. I will try the number "8".

Clank.

//Success!
Opening drawer to dispense 'Key'...

A drawer creaks open for me to retrieve the key. I grab it and bolt up the stairs. I wrap around the hallway and am met with yet another computer terminal. Around every corner, it feels as if my life is a circus of circuits. Hmm. There is indeed a play-on-words in there somewhere, the likes of which I am too embarrassed to attempt to conjure up.

Before I contemplate further whether I am losing my mind, I shall startup this device. I pressed the power button and waited a moment.

** Booted up **
"What would you like to do?"

My two options are as follows:

Data Station Manual

Configure Elevator.

I suppose it would benefit me to know what the manual dictates first. Let us start there. The computer screen reads,

//To startup the Data Station, follow this order:
(1) Turn first gauge to this number - 19
(2) Turn second gauge to this number - 45
(3) Press white button below gauges
(4) 5-digit code for dials - 1 3 5 7 9
(5) Flip the all the switches up below the dials
(6) Wait for audible sound then press the red button
** Should you correctly follow the command proper, you are now ready to use the Data-inator Mk. III! **

I guess there is some adjunct machine somewhere else? I look to my right, since this terminal sits in a corner with a wall to my left and its backside, and behind me is the way I came. I can see another similar device across the way.

In-between is another lobby that extends out to the left, if I am facing the new machine, from the hallway connecting the devices. I notice there is an elevator taped all over with caution tape. That means nothing to me anymore. I have begun to accept many-a-cautions in my life as it is, what would one more do to me? Am I becoming too numb?

I started up the Data Machine. It is asking for some input sequence to continue with booting up. As I recall, the machine earlier instructed me to turn the gauges first, press the white button, enter a code, and finally press the red button. Sounds simple enough. Here it goes.

//Select your operation. . .

>Configure Elevator Terminal

>Read off data entries

I elected to configure this terminal first. I turned the first gauge to 19 and the second to 43. A buzzing sound came from the machine. I primed the white button. External lights finally came on.

Upon the next prompt, I entered the code: 1-3-5-7-9. The terminal emitted a jarring, whirring sound.

At last, I depressed the red button. A chime was made.

Now, I will investigate the data entries to see what's really happened.

Here is what I found in the archives:

"1941-43 - Major Events:

<u>Dec. 1941:</u>

Unexpected tragedy on Pearl Harbor. Talk of future American involvement in the War immediately followed.

Jan. 1942:

The Manhattan Project is rushed to begin developing atomic weaponry. A new field of science began to unfurl as techniques arose for nurturing atomic fission.

Mar. 1942:

Scientists are unsure what to call the newly developing field. Eagerness awaits for one to father it.

1945 - The Turning Point:

<u>June 1945:</u>

As the project culminates for the newly innovated atomic bombs, two planes are designated for delivery.

<u>August 6, 1945:</u>

Planes for departure vanish along with the bombs. Locations unknown.

<u>August 6, 1945:</u>

Planes with bombs intended for Japanese cities instead drop on Paris and London. God help us. No one knows a thing.

1950s - A New Era:

<u>Feb. 1950:</u>

It has been nearly five years since the incident. Germany and Japan have taken over the world's technology by storm. They won. The States are in ruin. Everyone is now an enemy.

1958:

Nanotechnology, a science initially born in the 1940s, emerges as a newly announced and official science. Discoverer will not reveal his identity. All known sources indicate anonymity."

=== END OF DATA BANK ===

I find myself dumbfounded, staring blankly at the screen. Why does this seem so familiar? It feels like I have a history with nanotechnology. But how? Why? I am fumed up with bitterness and hatred! I know I remember! It's not there. I can't access my own memory!

I smashed the control board of the terminal and punched the screen. A couple sparks flew, the screen fizzled, and some smoke emitted. I've almost had it with these machines telling me what I do or do not know, or what I am supposed to or not supposed to know! Can't I just be that which I would like to become? Why must I conform to what has been, instead of what can be? Am I resisting something?

I shuffle my feet with my head low back to the first machine across the hallway. I choose to configure the elevator this time and enable it. A thunk was heard where the elevator was, and I proceeded to it. I tear away the tapings and press the down button on the wall panel. After a couple flickers, it fully lights up. I can audibly hear the gears and mechanical parts crunching and squeaking back into place.

The doors open only a quarter of the way, so I pried them open a little more for me to fit through them. Inside, I look for the floor selection panel. There are three options: 1F, 2F, and B. I figured 'B' stands for basement, and I've already regrettably visited the other two floors to some extent.

Aside from the factory operating area itself, I think what I need could be somewhere in the basement. About a second later from pressing the button, dissonant elevator music plays. It was the most horrible sound in the world. I mean, if I didn't know any better, you'd have a better chance of selling a hit record of nothing more than the sound of nails on a chalkboard than whatever was playing in this elevator.

I took my pistol and shot the speaker system.

Peace at last. A fleeting moment of relief.

Around a minute later, the elevator came to a screeching, agonizing stop. The doors tried their best to reopen, but they just slipped down a bit instead about halfway. I pry them the elevator doors open once more and shimmy through the crevice I made.

In the distance ahead I see a wall with two arched openings on either side. I go through the entrance on the left and discover a chest.

I open the chest to find a double-barrel shotgun. It hones the word "Wulfsinger" carefully carved into the side of its wooden barrel. Across the way looms two dimly lit, eye-resembling circles lurking in the shadows. The far wall is all but illuminated.

Dare I let my curiosity bang the gavel and drag me into this valley of hazardous peril? A cold chill hastily slithers down my spine and into the farthest reaches of my feet. Let's do this. I creep forward, walking at an angle. Closer and closer I tread.

I must have triggered a sensor, because lights above began to flicker before illuminating the area here.

The object turned out to be a large reddish-copper robot. Across its metallic chest is a Russian word it would seem.

It reads, "Осуждение". I brush off the dust around it with my hand. I revealed another word that is a smaller font but in English and what I presume to be its translation: "Condemnation".

I know that I need to acquire the component I came this far to get. Where did they put it in this anthropomorphic suit of nuts and bolts? It should be in a locked compartment in the chest or the upper back. I don't see any panel here in the front, but perhaps if I go around-The ground begins to quake slightly, sending me wobbling on one leg briefly. I restore my balance as it ends.

The robot's eyes light up a deep yellow. Its shutters blink twice at me. Metallic grunting and muffled talking comes from the robot.

"You have to get out of here," it said. Why does the robot sound like a gargled version of Rebekah's voice, as if it were transmitted through an iron tunnel?

"Excellent work bypassing the system." The voice of the robot changed into a male-sounding voice with deep undertones and metallic grating. Its eyes shutter and transition to dark red.

"You have given me access to the Factory's integrated system. All thanks to you, I can use the data to eradicate all profiles. Macht will be proud! However shall I repay you? Oh, I know! I'll start by eradicating you, just as I did with your beloved Ratiocinator!

"INTRUDER ALERT! MUST. BE. EXTERMINATED!" The robot begins to stand up, creaking and whining as its hydraulic pumps prime for the first time in who knows how long.

I reach for my Wulfsinger shotgun. It turns its magnificent torso to me. Every movement is accompanied by a whining, rattling sound. I am suddenly gazing down the triple barrel on top of its right arm.

This is a grenade launcher!

I dive forward and roll between its legs. The beast blasts anyway. I shoot the back of its left knee with my shotgun. Barely a dent. Its tremendous body jolts forward only a hair. It spins quickly, whacking me with a backhand to the wall with its left arm. The attachment for the left hand is a drill?! You've got to be kidding me.

Cocking back his left arm, he looks me dead in the eye. The drill furiously cycles. I barrel-roll to the side. Its drill impales the wall, sending chunks of concrete, plaster, and shrapnel everywhere. Sparks spew here and there. Condemnation raises its right foot and looks to stomp on me, but I shoot the sole of the contraption, knocking it onto its back.

I climb up its leg as it's falling, trying to reload my gun as I do. I managed to put two more shells into my shotgun. It tries to grab me with its other arm, but I mostly dodged just in time. It lightly scraped my right leg as I maneuvered, just enough to cause stinging and irritation, and instill a desire to blow its scrapyard head clean off its wretched body.

"Eddy, wait!" spoke the robot. I lowered my gun in awe. Its eyes turned yellow again.

"What about all the times we shared together?"

I don't recall ever giving this sentient junkyard my name? And what does it mean 'we'?

"Who are you?" I asked.

"Funny you should ask that, Eddy. I meant to ask you the same thing. Interesting how that works, Malcolm." Its eyes turned red again. As it fumbled to get back up again, I leaped off its chest and tumbled onto the ground.

"Annihilation is mandatory. Eddy Malcolm, prepare for recruitment." I am again looking down the triple barrel, my back to the ground, half-sitting up. Gun in my hand.

"You should have stayed back at the Lab, Eddy," Condemnation scoffed. I can see the ember glow at the end of the steel tunnel. Wait. That's it! Count it down, Eddy. I rushed my hands to my gun and pointed it at the horror awaiting me. Three, two... *NOW!!* I pulled the trigger the same time Condemnation released its grenade. BANG! Its arm exploded clean off, directing scraps everywhere. There's an opening now through its right side.

"Think about what you're doing, Eddy. We can help you get better," it said.

"Burn in your own flames!!" I roared back.

"Retaliation is futile. Join us. The power only gets stronger every day. One of us, Eddy. One of..." I fire my second shot between its infuriatingly stubborn robotic eyes.

"She's waiting, Eddy...Eurrghh...." The eyes fade out as its voice trails off. Its body collapses to the left side. I go around to the back and search for the control panel. I smash it open with the butt of my shotgun, and carefully tear up an opening so as not to cut myself on the jagged pieces.

There it is. The chip component. I detach it and tuck it into my inner coat pocket. As I walked away, I heard a faint rumbling behind me. I glance back to where the robot once lay, only to see that it's...

"REBEKAH?!" I cried. She's face down on the ground, faintly twitching, trying to call for me. The robot was completely gone. What is happening? "Eddy, come closer, I need to tell you something." She said softly, gesturing with a wave of her fingers. I stoop down to listen.

"Was this fantasy, or reality?" She asked.

"My dear, I-I don't-" I stuttered, dumbfounded by the prompt.

"Which is it, Eddy?" She asked one more time, this time more sternly, her eyes peering into my soul with a look of indignation.

"This was—reality." I replied.

"Thank you for releasing me, Eddy. Once again, the Resistance rises." Her body dematerializes like the crackles of a bonfire, in association with an accommodating wobbly chiming sound.

Parts of this area that once were color became monochromatic. This is the second time I have been visited by that particular question.

Was it actually reality? Or am I a fool beneath all reproach?

CHAPTER XII

BACK TO YOUR ROOTS

With the memory chip components from both Kathryn and now the ol' factory, that just leaves the office. That blasted firm. Am I technically visiting my future in the past? That's how Kathryn explained it to me, in my mind's eye. There are many things, I feel, that I am not being told and probably for my own benefit.

The air here is crisp, like a cool autumn day. I know the factory and the office are not too distant from each other. I'd say only a five mile journey, and I'm already a mile or so out from the factory. Perhaps I can take this time to collect myself for the upcoming trek. See the side of the road? All these hedges. Someone took the precious time to curate this species of greenery. And, since they still stand here as I speak, they had to have been cared for thus far. A cycle of tenderness. It's simple reciprocity. This makes me miss easier times.

However, I do not think the past was meant for dwelling in, but rather to reflect upon. I can take comfort in that. What has been is not equal to what will be, necessarily. Predictions come and go, but the state of my sanity definitely fluctuates from moment to moment. Wait, what? Is that how that goes? No, this is fine. I'll make it up as I go along, and there's no one here to stop me.

"Eddy! I found you!" a voice yelled from behind. Well, there's always tomorrow. I turned around.

"Kathryn!? However did you find me?"

"To make a short story long, the memory component I gave you serves as a tracker of sorts. Use that information how you will. But there's something we need to discuss."

"On the way, of course?" I gestured at the road.

"Yes, on the way, no less." She half-curtsied. We talked over what it meant to truly be content, among other things of life's intricate qualities. Quite the ice breaker, isn't it? The miles suddenly felt like mere yards. We now were within eyesight's reach of the old accounting firm.

I took a deep breath in before continuing. I know very well what lies beyond those putrid doors, the hollow halls, and the decadent cubicles. Pure deception, ethical disintegration, and fleeting cognizance—a zombification, if you will.

Out of the corner of my eye, I can see Kathryn's sympathetic look as she glances upon me. For a woman so fierce, she can be so tender. I admire that about her. Is it selfish that I'd long for Rebekah to be by our side as well? I haven't told Kathryn yet about Rebekah. I think that she believes Rebekah is still out there, and I don't have the heart or wisdom to tell her what I saw back at the hospital. The...hospital.... The.... I feel woozy.

"Eddy! Eddy?! Come back, you're here with me. Everything's fine." Kathryn snaps her fingers. No response from me, it doesn't seem close enough to wake me up. Finally she slapped me metaphorically into next week, though it felt quite literal.

"Pull yourself together, man! Our intel shows that this office is abandoned. It's just going to be the two of us. We go in, get the component, and be on our merry way."

"Right, you're right." I gulped.

"C'mon, let's get this rat-infested memory over with." This ramshackle firm stands about 8 stories, vines reaching as high as the fifth floor. The glass front doors are cracked with bullet holes here and there. I can affirm that no one would notice if the building's discourse were left to spontaneous combustion, if you catch my proverbial powder keg.

"Careful, Eddy. One little huff or puff and it might blow the entire building down," joked Kathryn.

"Hilarious, but true. And how unfortunate if it did, am I right?" I retaliated with a chuckle. We climbed to the second floor using the ramshackled staircase that has been out of commission, as it were, for many-a-year. At its end, the staircase has a hallway parallel to it, similar to what was at Zero Naught.

"We sure have a thing for run-down buildings and staircases, don't we, Kathryn?" I teased. She rolled her eyes and shook her head in exasperation. We are greeted by an open floor. There's a room to the left, to the right. We go to the room to the right. In this room are a couple computer units spanning about half the far wall. The interior walls have filing cabinets and desks. There is a maze of desks and person-sized shelves throughout the middle of the room.

We work our way counterclockwise from the doorway. Cabinet after cabinet we sorted. Some of the cabinets randomly appear to be colored black-and-white. Again? Why does this feel familiar? The trees, that road sign, the chair. What do these all have in common? Why the blanks?

After a few minutes, I remained fruitless in my endeavors. We decided to split up to cover more ground. In here? Nothing. Over there? Negative. Oh!? Wait, nope, false alarm. It looked vaguely interesting, but I digress from my mission.

"Eddy, take a look at this." beckoned Kathryn. I marched delicately over to her. She pointed to the name she found in the cabinet. Can it really be?

"Okami's file," I grumbled. We give each other that look of affirmation and nod. We must open it. I grab it out of the filing cabinet and drop it on the desk. It is a typical manila folder, with his name colored and outlined in a red rectangle. A picture of him is attached by paperclip to the top-front.

The string "PH-HI-43" is stamped below his name. That sounds vaguely familiar.... Kathryn read aloud the details of the file,

"Everything we know about Yakeru 'Okami' Nishimura: the Flaming Wolf from the Western Village. Threat level: insurmountable. Age: unknown. Date of birth: 1894, reportedly. Height: 1.8 meters. Eye color: unknown, always wears helmet. Do not engage, ever. Known by his coat with fur-lined collar."

I know that imagery from somewhere. Pearl Harbor? Was he there? Think, Eddy! He was there, wasn't he? James warned you to take cover, then Okami said, "Don't worry, Doctor. You two will meet again in hell, I'm sure." And he threw James's dead body at my feet. HE WILL PAY FOR THAT!! Kathryn is noticing my anger as I'm sure the tension is very visible in my face.

"Eddy, what is it? What happened? Was it another flashback?" She asked. I grit my teeth and clench my jaw and try to collect myself, but it's not working. I'm only getting more and more worked up over it.

"I want him dead, Kathryn. He killed James! I was there! Pearl Harbor, December 1941! That was him, that was Okami! He's responsible for the deaths of all my brothers!!" I yelled.

"Eddy, he's getting inside your head! You'll get your chance, but we can't risk it right now! Try to think!" Kathryn said, trying to give calming gestures to me. I take a few deep breaths. I can feel the tension leaving my arms and my blood pressure coming back down. I am... calm? Is that what this feels like?

"Eddy, I'm going to read a little bit more so we know what we are up against, alright? We need to do this, it could be our only chance!" I am still recovering from my outburst. I have that zoned-out feeling as I try to control my breathing. Focus is a five-letter word put as far from me as the gallows are to the grave. The principle remains the same in my mind. Take it or leave it to the ground to be burned to ashes.

"Okay. Continue. I can do this," I finally said, still taking deep breaths from my gut.

"The background of Yakeru Nishimura: Okami is a military commander in Japan's armed forces. He has been heading their science division since the start of this second Great War. All we know so far is that there is talk about merging ideas with German scientists to develop a device capable of recruiting hundreds of thousands of soldiers at will. We must act swiftly and fiercely. This unruly evil must be stopped before it's too late. Last known location of Okami: unknown. Reports of a secret laboratory somewhere in central Europe. No further details at this time. Godspeed."

That was the end of the file. No known leads. Why is Okami so intent on working this closely with Macht? Something's missing.

"Hey, Eddy, there's a crumbled-looking piece of paper tucked within the pages. Let's check it out together. Alright. It's hard to read but I think it says, 'Akihiro Nishimura: Father of Yakeru, Friend to contemporary engineer Walter Kysh. Spouse: Cho 'Blossom' Nishimura. Last known location of Akihiro: Paris, France.' Hm.

"Do you know why that would have been included in Okami's file? And why would it be hidden?" asked Kathryn.

My eyes sprung open as never before.

"Is everything okay?" she asked.

"Yeah, yeah. It's just that... Walter Kysh... was my grandfather," I said, astonished.

Kathryn gasped and nearly dropped the file.

"While I'm thinking about it, sometimes I do wonder if my father's weird condition was passed down to me to any extent.

That would make much sense and explain a great deal, " I said under my breath.

I shrugged my shoulders and quickly changed subjects.

"What do we do, Kathryn?" I asked.

"I'll tell you what we're not gonna do. We're not-" she starts to reply.

"What, what, what are you doing in here?!" shouted a voice from behind, interrupting Kathryn. We hear mechanical-like footsteps, clanking rapidly with steam-sputtering sounds as well.

"What the devil?" I whispered to Kathryn.

"Eddy, we gotta go," said Kathryn.

"Agreed." I grabbed Okami's folder and tucked it inside my coat.

"Hey, hey! W-who invited you-you lot here? Here?!" cried the voice. A silhouette stood at the doorway. We raised our guns.

"Show yourself or be shot! First and only warning!" yelled Kathryn.

"Show-show myself? Ha-ha, ah-ah! I will show YOU. This is, this is a warning! Test, t-test! Code GREEN!" stammered the voice.

"What's wrong with this guy? Something's off about the way he's talking. I don't like it," I said.

The person walks through the doorway and into the light. He has a face that not even a nursing mother could love. It is misshapen and contorted with burn marks. His goggles are all broken, and he has these two robotic appendages coming from some attachment on his waist. His mouth and eyes are twitching rather frequently and showing a violent hippus reaction.

"Why, hello!" His head twitches to the side. "Allow me to introduce myself. I am D-Doctor Jorax. And you-you are?"

There are two gas-fueled cylindrical vats and an indicator light attached to Jorax's back, and the green ooze inside the vats is lightly bubbling.

"Leaving. We were just leaving." prompted Kathryn.

"I was going to say 'intruders', but I'm glad we are all on the same page. I think you've read too much of my collection as it is." Jorax fires up the two vats by pressing a detonator in his right hand. The ooze begins to furiously froth and bubble now. The tops of them rattle like a tea kettle, and the froth pours over, dripping down the sides and onto the tile floor.

"Eddy?" said Kathryn.

"Kathryn?" I asked.

"Let's run," she said.

"Let's," I emphasized. We bolted off in opposite directions towards the walls and tried to get around Jorax.

"I don't think-think so-RRRAARARA!" chuckled Jorax. The indicator light is now on. He unsheathes a longsword from his side and lights it on fire from the dripping ooze he's collected. The fire is green as well. Jorax tries to swing at me but misses completely, stabbing a desk.

"Hey, 'Borax'! Had too much to drink, have we? I'm over here!" I taunted.

"Your feeble-feeble efforts. Efforts?? Are of no purpose to me. Wait. Me? YOU have mistaken the wrong guy for death!" raged Jorax. Kathryn chuckled under her breath.

"Eddy," she wheezed, "I-I can't take him seriously, but we seriously have to make a run for it, before he can actually land a hit!"

"Oh no, you d-d-d-don't! I have collected all the IRAG grenades, and I'm not afraid-afraid of using them!! *Comme c'est terrible!* G-get some while they're fresh!" Kathryn and I stop in our tracks as we're almost out the door, while Jorax is still figuring out how to get unstuck from the desk. I take out my pistol and shoot one of his vats, leaking hot, boiling ooze over him. The indicator light is now blinking.

"RRAAARHGHGH. AAHHHHG! You will see an end-end to your days soon! I-I-my schematics are always. ...?!? Right!!"

"Tell us about those IRAGS, or I'll shoot out the other one, Doc." I cocked my pistol again, pointing the barrel straight at the remaining vat.

"L-listen, Eddy. Is it? It is! So I've heard from your alleged wife here-here. H-here's the thing that's so special about... th-those IRAG grenades. BOOM, boom!!"

Kathryn and I exchange exaggerated looks of confusion. Jorax slaps the emergency button on his chest. The vats wind down and the appendages retract. He inhales deeply and breathes steadily.

"Besides the fact I modified them to Macht's specifications," his voice and eyes both relax, "I added a little surprise to one out of every 5 that I made." Jorax finally retrieved his longsword from the desk, and starts walking toward us.

"Yes, there's a chance that when one of those go off, it will release so much heat that everything around it within a 15-foot radius melts and burns to ashes! *Tres bien!*"

"You're insane!!" cried Kathryn. Jorax's face becomes expressionless, suggesting annoyance at something clearly accurate.

"Insanity is so vague. They tell you to conform. What of it when you don't? I am forever criminalized, forced to hide now. I live here, keeping the archives of all who've fallen under Macht and Okami, and all that will. It's just that the archives are almost complete. I am missing only one name." Jorax checks a digital log on some device on his forearm.

"Do either of you, by complete happenstance, know an 'Edward J. Malcolm'?" asked Jorax with a smirk.

Kathryn turned white. We don't say anything.

"So you do. Pray tell, I would like to meet him. I have a present for him from Macht himself. A super-special IRAG grenade just for him." said Jorax.

On his backside, I see a sort of control panel. Perhaps, if I can knock it out, it should destabilize his arsenal.

"Let's say I'm this Eddy Malcolm you're looking for. What would you do?" I procured. "Simple. Total annihilation. But you wouldn't understand. He is guilty of over 317 different war crimes. Justice is long overdue, according to Macht," replied Jorax.

Kathryn casts a horrendous glance at me and looks at Jorax in disgust. "And you know, what else? I think that-"

"Eddy, now!" exclaimed Kathryn. I barrel-roll and shoot the back control panel from the side in an attempt to not kill Jorax, only to weaken him for answers. His systems shut down, and he collapses to his knees then gradually sits down, scooting himself against the wall, juices leaking as he does.

"Jorax, listen well. I am Eddy Malcolm, and don't you forget. My goal is to end Macht and restore this world," I said firmly.

"So you are Eddy, but are you the 'Baron Rogue'? What do I care, anyway? I'm just a prisoner, you know that? My only purpose to live right now is to protect these archives, so they don't kill me themselves. They're coming for me now, I just know it. The records have been compromised." Jorax pauses briefly.

"Listen, I need you to do me a favor, Eddy. You have to shoot the other vat, while it's hot. I-I can't go out a failure. They took everything from me." Jorax's voice breaks. He starts up the vats again, tears streaming down his cheeks.

"Jorax, you can't do this! There's a way out!" said Kathryn.

"No. This is me, and this is how I need to go. I am over my overthinking. I will finally be free. I am...free. To be me." Jorax smiles. He takes his sword, lights it on fire again with one of the many devices hooked up to him, and stares at us, his eyes as red as a sunset.

"You need to go. You have to go and stop Macht and Okami. It can be done. You're going to need my lab. It's back at Zero Naught. Someone will meet you there."

"Jorax, what?" I asked.

"Go, Eddy. GO!!" He said.

Kathryn and I booked it out of there. We heard a fire ignite, lowered our heads, and proceeded to the staircase at the other end of the floor. The split second we made it out of the building, an explosion came from the room of the floor we were at with Jorax.

He did it. He freed himself from Macht's nigh-inescapable grasp. It shouldn't have come down to this, but it did. We cried. We felt so hopeless. What could we even have done differently? It finally clicked with us that Jorax must've been brainwashed to do Macht's dirty work. This has to be the work of an IRAG. We will avenge you, Jorax!

"Eddy, I must at last do it. Go back to the lab, we'll meet up soon," said Kathryn.

"Huh? Where are you going? And how?" I asked.

"I'm going to learn more about what we are up against, straight from the source. And, a woman has her ways for getting what she wants," said Kathryn with a gratuitous wink.

CHAPTER XIII
THE FORGING OF A BROTHERHOOD

Meanwhile in Eastern Europe, in the far reaches of the empire's cornerstone, Okami and Macht were establishing plans for their final move from inside their Castle *des Fluss* (of the river). That is, it is established upon land by a most gravitating, most eloquent river.

The castle in question is a magnificent structure flaunting the purest white bricks. Golden crenelations across the top of the walls stand equidistant from each other, painting the rays of a granite sunset. Four turrets bulwark the corners of the keep. The back two turrets stand taller than the front two as part of their amalgamation with the Romanesque Cathedral of Saint Peter. A majestic mahogany gate in the front of the castle easily opens for its citizens. Three crimson, well-adorned banners on either outside wall adjacent to the gate drape with distinguished impetus.

Surrounding the outside castle grounds is a moat spanning the length of a two score and ten meters. Its gauzy waters diverge on either side of its arched bridge, which was built as a continuation of the Remagen Bridge, composed of the smoothest gray stone brick of late-gothic design. If one were to follow its treacherous path, it could be seen that its many canals converge into the twisting River Rhine.

Sweet Loreley, that graceful queen of the river, lies not too, too far away. Roughly, 77 klicks. Legends tell of the many sailors that have tried to woo her waves but have fallen to the harrowing sirens that desire their gold and souls even more. It is unknown to this day the last time its lighthouse was in operation. Macht evaded the sirens' seductions, though his appearance fair suggests varying tales, by not having regard to entertain the glittering waters which taunt the vessels that do traverse its streams. His desire for unity had no quarrel with tantalizing temptresses. He remembered well the last time he tried to think about even a remote interest in love or any form of the idea or anything other than what he was created to be. Yearning for acceptance was never satisfiable, he thought, so yearning shall cease to be.

In the throne room of their beloved castle, Macht and Okami are simply waiting. The week's deadline is nearing its end.

A royal messenger entered the room, transcript in hand.

"Macht, we have received word that two of our guardians have fallen to Eddy and his rogue order," she said.

"Hmph. So they have. You know, it is interesting how you try to steer someone astray, and they find out the truth in the process. Knowing this poetry, my anger is deterred. For now. Now, who exactly did we lose?"

"We lost Condemnation and Jorax," she stated. Macht jolts.

"Uh, eheh. What?" he returned a deadpan question. "How, pray tell, could my loyal, indiscriminate machines fail me?"

"I think there's a field of weakening when Eddy is within range," added Okami, "The more he realizes the Baron Rogue Proper, the stronger the resistance. Macht, if he gets to us, and we can't stop him—"

"OF COURSE WE'LL STOP HIM!!" shouted Macht, more than visibly frustrated. He adjusts his attire back into its formalities. "Ahem, when we complete the final phase, we need not worry anymore about him."

The messenger left the room discreetly.

"Macht, with all due respect, you have yet to disclose this 'final phase' to me. If I am to carry it out efficiently, it would behoove you to share."

"You know how every time we capture someone's memories, we were able to use it to increase our cerebral processing power, or, as someone else pointed out, our 'intelligence quotient'? As soon as we successfully harness Eddy's mind, we will be set to live forever."

"As promising as living forever sounds, how do we prosper from it?" Okami asked.

"It is simple. The longer we live, the more we can realize our full potential and innovations. In my world, everyone is under my fist. This new world of mine, formed by science alone, will seal everyone to the same destiny of unity," answered Macht.

"I'll play the devil's advocate one more time: what if I do not desire to live forever as you?" asked Okami.

"Whosoever does not desire to live forever is as good as dead. And what a terrible fate that death and its harbinger brings," replied Macht.

"So our life essence runs off the premise of an integrated database which is everybody's memory. And what if Eddy wins and destroys it?"

"It matters not. You see, I am unable to lose. We have yet to infuse ourselves with a critical component. Once we have assimilated in that manner, only one thing remains, which is determination to finish the race. If we lose, the death is two-fold. If I win, death is no more. Will you follow me, Okami?"

"To the end, brother," responded Okami who proceeded to leave the room. Macht, left to himself in this moment, as most moments afford, began to think aloud.

"Oh, father… Your grooming familiarity with chaos must be soothing to your wretched soul. So predictable of you. Like a dog returning to its emesis, you find yourself coming back for more.

"I wonder, how does it feel when you finally get that brief moment of harmony? Does it feel like uncertainty? Perhaps we have something in common after all. Maybe we are, in fact, the same, hm? Quite a revelation, I know." Macht turned to the closest object and smashed it with his reinforced gauntlets.

"I must improve, I have to! URGHH!! CURSE YOU, EDDY!! If you wanted to go to war so badly, then why didn't you in the first place?!" Macht slumped against the wall and slid into a sitting-up position on the floor. "Is my misery even curable, my anger satiable? A river of woe and sorrow am I; its waters are my only comfort. Resist I may, fight I must, but forever onward I shall drive the nails of regret further into the mind of Eddy Malcolm. When the very last one has been secured in its metallic crypt, the house of torment finally constructed, I will live forever! Forward, ever forward, always progressing. When at last I have completed every progression, rest shall come."

Macht stood back up.

"But now, now is the deciding moment. I will win, Eddy, whether you like it or not. Just be ready for your absolute defeat. My addiction to chaos is refreshing to my bitter soul."

A cleverly-disguised Kathryn has infiltrated into the castle and met up with Okami. After a few moments of conversation, Okami, unsuspecting, obliged to tell her the history of his story.

"So Okami, how did you and Macht meet?"

"We were told about this American soldier who had been caught with contraband in Germany. His name tag read 'Edward Malcolm.' I knew that name and the face with the name. That was not Doctor Malcolm. While Macht resembles Eddy, they are not at all the same person."

"He resembles Eddy? In what way?"

"Patience. I will explain everything. They exiled this 'Edward Malcolm' to a remote, broken down prison in Austria that was built right after the *Anschluss* happened. You could say Germany wanted a housing space for hostages to decide their fate at a later time. Every day was another tick on those prisoners' clock.

"Macht was not like the other prisoners. You see, since the real Edward Malcolm was a coward, Macht instead possessed all of the brutal traits that a warrior does. That is all he knew. Macht only knows war and how to win it. That is why he was created."

"Created?!" cried Kathryn, almost out-of-character.

"Hush. You interrupt me, mortal," said Okami, unsuspecting so far.

"Macht was captured because he had wandered too deep into enemy lines. He was left alone, abandoned by his battalion. That didn't bother him. As he had once told me, being alone is a sort of freedom for him. When he is alone, his thoughts provide him company as they flow one after the other. Macht encountered some trouble in his wandering. German patrol officers caught him. He wasn't doing anything, he was at ease, just observing... contemplating. But given the state of the world at the time, that is a death sentence. Total bloodshed was not in place yet, since Macht hadn't carried out his plan then, so he was given one more chance at life in that 'Prison for the Offensive'. Really, it was more like a forced labor camp.

"What did they do to him?" she asked.

"Terrible question. You should have asked, 'What did Macht do to them?' His first day revolutionized the meaning of the word 'revolt.' It was a prison break that was never quite witnessed before in modern Germany.

"First, Macht used some flint to carve into the wall with the window in his prison cell. During what-you-could-call their daily lunch time, food was not on Macht's mind. He gradually stole various kitchen utensils and hid them all very well in his outfit. While back out in the heat of the camp, he managed to obtain some socks in the ground. No guard questioned it, and they let him keep them.

"Later that night, Macht managed to use the socks as twine along with shoelaces he stripped off a fellow inmate, and tied two of the steak knives he obtained on opposite ends."

"That is great and all, but how does that help him escape?"

"That's the thing. The fact he was able to pull off his escape with just that overnight is almost unbelievable. With the flint markings on the wall, he created a fire in the mortar by using residue from pipes, cigars, and any other 'fuel' he found. With his other utensils, he created a trap above the door that would cause them to impale the first person to walk through. He saved the last knife as ammo for a crossbow he made from leftover twine and wooden spoons. With the steak knives, he carved the bricks out one by one until he created an opening that he could crawl through.

"Macht was on his last brick when he overheard guards talking about how the kitchen staff complained about missing items, and they were going to go through each cell to investigate. To make matters worse, the smell of the fire basically created a trail for the guards. At the time, Macht couldn't speak much German. While they were busy yelling at him and trying to open his door, he stood there, crossbow hidden behind his back, and witnessed his plan unfold. The first guard was killed by the door trap. Macht used his crossbow to get the second guard. He grabbed the handgun off the corpse and rushed out through the gap he created in the wall."

"How did he escape the guard towers?"

"Since the prison was so run-down, there were no guard towers to even occupy. It was presumed that no one could survive the prison's conditions, let alone escape to tell the story. Macht got away clean and escaped to a cottage to the East. It was there that I found him months later when I was given a mission by the Emperor after he heard about this clever American that outsmarted German mandates. Perhaps he could've been convinced, so to say, to pursue other aspirations, if you will.

"So, after many grueling weeks of analyzing whatever traces he left, I had finally found him. One other Japanese officer and I captured him in that cottage. He was enjoying his lunch, probably stolen. However, he was also hard at work on a device. Since I speak English, per my abroad education, I asked him what it was for. He did not respond, only grinned."

"What did you do to him?"

"I personally did nothing, but my idiotic supporting officer slapped him and yelled an unforgivable curse in Japanese. Macht is nearly two meters tall, you see, and has the muscle build of a mountain. Angering him would have been a firestorm of its own. Macht did not return hostility, but the glare he gave my comrade made him shut up and hide behind me.

"I asked him again what the device did. He finally answered, but not with what I wanted. Or, that is, with what I understood at the time.

"'If I told you,' he said, 'humanity will collapse faster than anticipated.' Of course, I had no idea what this meant. My comrade charged once more at Macht but I shot my comrade for it when his back was turned to me.

"The smile on Macht's face told me enough. I introduced myself. But he knew who I was already. After that, he greeted me with 'Hello, Wolf. I am Macht: the Power Unforeseen.' We could tell that this was the beginning of something viciously beautiful."

"Just like that, Okami?"

"Precisely like that." Okami said.

"What device was he working on?"

"His first IRAG grenade."

"So that was the first after all? How do they work, exactly?"

"It absorbs the memories of whoever is within range and replaces them with only knowledge of war, if lucky. The victims don't even know their own names. They only know killing. That way, they feel the lifelong pain Macht has known. So his pain, and I quote, 'is relieved.'"

"What is that pain? Why does he go through all this effort to complete his plan?"

"Because Edward Malcolm was careless and a coward! He created Macht to go to war for him. How ironic if you ask me. The poor pitiful fool that is Eddy still found his way to the battlefield, an arrangement beautifully crafted by Macht. There is no escape from destiny. It will arrive, no matter what measures you take to avoid it. I am destiny. We are here." Okami stood up.

"And now, you get to witness history. We are rewriting it for the greater good of us all. It will be done. It cannot be stopped."

"What is the goal?"

"To erase Malcolm and to create peace and harmony. This is the only way to achieve unity."

"How do you know that?" aggressively asked Kathryn. Okami turned to Kathryn.

"You dare question the great Okami?!"

"N-no! I would never, I--" Okami grabbed Kathryn by the throat.

"Listen. This goes beyond you. It's something bigger than anything we've ever dreamed. Now, if you want to live, spy, it's best to not ask anymore questions." Okami released his grip.

"Y-You won't be able to stop E-Eddy!" stuttered Kathryn, coughing and gasping for breath on the ground.

"He has been stopped already. He sealed his own fate long ago. What a fool. And to believe you actually followed him. And now, I have no choice but to make you a puppet. With stakes like these, you'll bring the gambler Eddy right to us," grinned Okami, crouching to her befallen level.

"I can't wait to tell Macht all about you."

CHAPTER XIV
DIMENSIONLESS PROTOCOL

I made it back to Zero Naught. Finally, I have all the pieces needed to fully assemble the memory chip. Jorax mentioned something about his lab being around here and that someone will also meet us there. But where, and who? Not too long after, I am approached by someone who does not seem too intrigued with talking, at least at length. The upper right side of the chest has a patch that reads the numbers "317" and the upper left has one with the numbers "0116". His steel-clad knightley-tiered armor is well-trimmed with gold and red decor.

"Hello there, do you know of the whereabouts of a laboratory that this whack-job called Jorax talked about?" I asked.

"I am the Warden, you may not pass. I am the only occupant here. Access to my lab is prohibited to all," replied the Warden.

"Excuse me, your lab?" I asked offensively.

"That is what I said, no? You will do well to leave at once!"

"That's it! I've had it!!" Eddy pulled his gun and shot the Warden, but the bullet dissolved into thin dust around him.

"Perhaps you did not hear me. I AM. THE WARDEN!" proclaimed the Warden.

"What…what is this?" I asked myself, frightened by this turn of events.

The Warden withdrew with his right hand a fanciful weapon that resembled a lance on one end and a magic staff on the other. The staff end had a glowing sphere attached. It is currently glowing yellow.

"I believe you do not understand how this universe works. I have been given a grand power by Power himself," said The Warden.

"Macht…." I said gruntingly.

"As his enemies would call him, yes. But his fidel proselytes have greater respect for his will. I will teach you why." The sphere changed from a slow-breathing yellow to a sharp red. The Warden took aim and blasted red energy at my feet, blowing me back a few meters. Several tumbles scraped me up. I have no idea how to counter this. If this is another one of Macht's doings, then it must follow some pattern from the previous fights. The sphere changed again from red to a steadily flashing blue.

The Warden fired blasts around me that caused the surrounding ground to ripple and wave, like I was a ship out at sea. I am tossed back and forth, rocks knocking me this way and that. Again, WHAT IS THIS?! I take the components of my memory chip and try to assemble them.

"I don't think so!!" denied The Warden. Now the sphere is a forest green. The Warden flipped the weapon and stabbed the ground with the lance end. Roots erupted toward me. They pierced the corrupted soil and wrapped my ankles and hands and locked me down. Any sort of movement was unachievable, and the memory chip parts collapsed from my hand to the ground. The Warden used the staff to propel himself to my position.

"Why are you doing this?" I asked, struggling to break free from my earthy cuffs. The Warden spun his weapon and speared the earth at his side to rest it there. He takes a long look at me.

"It is you, isn't it Eddy?" he asked me.

"And you gathered that conclusion how?" I asked him.

"I know the Baron Rogue when I see him, but I didn't think he'd be this easy to capture. To think you were going to take down Macht. HA! To be seeing me just now means you're out of time. This will be over quickly, I'll spare him valuable time by ending you myself." The Warden picked up his weapon and aimed the sphere at me; it's swirling with the four colors. It's whirring, spinning, changing to an intense white. I can feel the heat overcoming me as it charges.

All of a sudden, a bullet blasts the weapon in half. The Warden looked over to the direction of the firing. I smiled. It was the same people from Rebekah's meeting room. They came!

"Commandants of the 317, ATTACK!!" roared the Ratiocinator. They started firing away at his armor but there was a shield of dimensional energy preventing the bullets from piercing through.

"You!! You're supposed to be dead, you little hellion!" roared The Warden.

"Name's Marshall, actually, but I like the sound of that too!" scoffed the Ratiocinator. The Warden unsheathed his flail into his left hand and summoned the former weapon to reassemble in his right hand. He propelled himself forward with his staff into the oncoming brigade. The roots that once held me crumbled after he advanced a certain distance. Now I know the rules at least have a spatial component to them.

I assembled my memory chip during this distraction. I know it isn't finished without the power source battery, but if I can somehow give it enough juice, I might be able to use it against The Warden. Amidst the conflict, I can see the sphere emitting sparks, be it ethereal or electric, I will take my chances. It looked like his shield didn't take kindly to bullets, but his weapon appeared to have no problem breaking and repairing.

I believe there to be a window of contingency in which to execute my plan. I see the struggle race onward, people fighting my battle. No, NO! I can't do this again!! I need to stand my ground, I need… I NEED TO FIGHT BACK!!! I sprinted toward The Warden with all I had, the memory chip in my left fist. I was ready to strike from the backside. He turned his head toward me as I wound my punch.

"Oh, please," he sympathized. He whacked me with his arm and knocked me aside.

"FOR EDDY!!" the brigade uproared. A formation was formed.

"317!!!" shouted Marshall.

"FOR GLORY!!" The brigade launched a synchronous barrage of gunfire at The Warden. He resisted with his energy shield and pushed back but it was slowly breaking from the forces of resolution.

Now is my chance! With The Warden distracted, I climbed back up from the ground and snatched the lancer-staff. Without another second of hesitation, I charged my memory chip with the staff. The most glorious reaction occurred. All around me I could see half the objects, natural and artificial alike, transition their colors into a black-and-white, but the other half was unphased. The primary colors rapidly filled my completed memory chip.

When the reaction finished, the color was a uniform, pure white. The Warden's shield shattered instantly.

Everyone stopped to stare at me. I noticed there was a slot in the weapon I wielded. I can see my memory chip fitting perfectly in there. "

Don't do it, Eddy… You don't have the competency, you will deteriorate in seconds!!" said The Warden to deter me.

"Maybe, maybe not. But I have a feeling that my chance of winning lies with this. If not, I can certainly get there."

"Don't you see it? This war could never be won. No one will win. You don't stand a chance. You and your militia will be absolutely decimated."

"At least I'd be able to say that I tried! I tried to right all my wrongs!" I said, pointing to himself.

"And that will be all that there ever will be! One effort after another. I'm sure," retorted The Warden.

"Warden, listen to me, listen! You're letting Macht get inside your head! Fight it!" I exclaimed.

"It's too late, Eddy. I'm already gone," he said.

"What?!" I cried. The Warden pulled out an IRAG grenade from the backside of his armor.

"EVERYONE, get down and look away!!"

"IRAG!!" shouted Marshall. I used the weapon to blast myself away to safety.

"I am so terribly sorry for this...." The Warden detonated the grenade in front of his own face. His body collapsed like a marionette whose strings just got cut. Perhaps that was genuinely the case.

"Another day, another mind..." said Marshall.

"Hey Marshall, I remember when I fought this robot, it said you were terminated? Wanna kindly tell me about how you are, in fact, not dead?"

"Heh. Well, I have a complicated hatred toward death, as it were, but in short, I made a deal."

"A deal? With whom? About what?"

"Listen, fellow. Sometimes in life you just have to make a sacrifice play, and let me be the first to tell you, sometimes it isn't fun!!" exclaimed Marshall.

"Well... that certainly brings up more questions than it actually answers, but would you be so kind as to share your great escape?"

"Oh, well why didn't you say so!" perked up Marshall.

"Great, here we go again, boys!" echoed the brigade.

"Lend an ear, Cap'n, for the great escape of Marshall the Great! Ready? Here goes... I hid in a pocket of spacetime!"

"...Funny, but seriously, how?" I asked.

"Read my lips, ya bewildered star sailor! You remember when you saw some things turn black and white? Welp, I discovered that if you hide with that object, your existence is nonexistent in that specific pocket. Ergo,..." Marshall shrugged his shoulders with outstretched open hands.

"Ergo, you were 'dead'!" I said.

"Precisely, my boy! Let's get to that lab, we have work to do," invited Marshall.

"Wait," stopped Eddy, "what about Rebekah then?" Marshall paused in his march, turned around, smiled and winked at him, then continued onward and forward.

Back at Castle *des Fluss*, things were not as jubilant. In their own regard, one could say, the politics were heating beyond the boiling point. Macht was ready for action and on the brink of global desiccation. In the meeting room of Macht and Okami, there was a singular question looming in their minds: When? Eddy and the 317 Brigade were prepping for all-out war. For the first time, it could have been said that worry had settled into the mind of Macht. Failure was an outcome not known by him. Determination filled the room, but the eagerness was incomprehensibly lacking.

"Okami. Pray tell, what numbers are displaying on the screen right now, under our names?" Macht's gaze was fixed on something in the distance in front of him, not even in the direction of Okami.

"Under your name, I see '512,' and under mine, I see '490'," stated Okami.

"And you remember what these numbers mean?"

"Our lifeforce, a banner of heraldry exhibiting our great minds. Our intelligence quotients, respectively. What of them?"

"And you know what happens if they reach zero?"

"We...cease to exist?" "That is correct, Okami. If we don't have Eddy's memory chip, we cannot stabilize this lifeforce."

"So what do we do?" asked Okami. A messenger came rushing into the room.

"Masters! We just received news that The Warden Proper has been freed!"

"By whom?!" asked Macht angrily.

"Our analysis shows that he did this himself," hesitated the messenger.

"What did the final moments show?" asked Okami.

"The last footage of the spectral camera in the staff showed that he used an IRAG to free himself, but in his vicinity was...um... the B-Baron Rogue." Macht slammed the table with his fists, causing the table to split apart.

"He knows...." whispered Macht.

"Leave us, please," requested Okami.

"Yes, Höchster Führers," replied the messenger, leaving the room at once.

"Okami, you asked what we should do. Try this on for size: find us a way to cross between dimensions. I wish to see everything. I want to see it all. I want full command," ordered Macht.

"Macht, I'm not sure even we have the molecular integrity to withstand that protocol," cautioned Okami.

"You're right. We do not, but I do. I am not as mortal as you, in a sense. That is, my molecules have a certain...give," said Macht with a menacing look.

"I'll get started right away," agreed Okami, who proceeded to leave the meeting room.

"I gave you a chance, Eddy. Now, I'm taking it away, with full prejudice," said Macht to himself.

CHAPTER XV

HIS BATTLEFIELD

The 317 brigade found themselves at Jorax's laboratory. Edward Malcolm, Marshall the Great, and the rest of the crew are standing about a round table with a schematic unfolded for all to see. The remainder of the story will now be told from the perspective encompassing the Baron Rogue.

"Here's what we currently know. Rebekah is presumed dead, Kathryn is MIA, and all hope is lost-" Marshall's voice choked up, and he began to cry.

"Hey, Marshall the Great Ratiocinator, I know we are all heartbroken, but they would have wanted us to keep going. We gotta try!" said Eddy, short-living his friend's time to mourn. The rest of the brigade had mixed responses amongst themselves.

"We can't apply logic to that which disagrees with logic. Let the man share his emotions!" sprouted one of the men.

"Interesting choice of words, Barrett. I think emotions are logical, they serve as the healthy link between the rational brain and the fluid soul, do they not? For what is a man without that which represents the being?" chimed in another.

"Yeah, Eddy, how can we experience release without attaching to the physical?" asked Barrett. All eyes except Marshall's, for personal reasons, were magnetized to Eddy's countenance.

"You will have to pardon me, then, gentlemen. It seems I have been astray until this point in my life. My eyes see clearly now the distinction," said Eddy.

"Okay. Okay,... I can do this. I just gotta... Okay. Ahem," said Marshall. "What we know is that these space-time pockets seem to be isolated fragments that permit a person, with the proper knowledge, to hide from the rest of the observable universe, while inside the quantum pocket. It stands to reason that, if your quantum state is unobserved inside this unobservable pocket, you don't exist inside that pocket, among other things," explained Marshall confidently.

"Therefore, we could launch a coordinated assault using these interdimensional foxholes. Do we know where the pocket locations are? Do we have a map?" asked Eddy.

"Well," Marshall thought for a moment, "if there is a link between your memory chip and the pattern of behavior with them, we could use that as a radar, theoretically from anywhere."

"Then let's try it right here, right now," insisted Eddy.

They set up the lancer-staff over the blueprints on the roundtable and connected the weapon to a broadcasting machine developed by Marshall. Eddy inserted his memory chip into the slot in the handle of the weapon. The entire room grew dim a second as the weapon absorbed the energy, the lights flickering once, maybe twice. The original lighting returned.

"Initializing broadcast in 3... 2... Go!" Marshall flipped the switch on his device. A screen was used to display pulsing and blips. The results were random, to say the least, but they revealed a critical detail:

"These pockets appear to be...almost global! Haha!" said Marshall. Eddy takes a closer look.

"No, not quite... They are appearing only in places I have visited, I think? I vaguely remember, but I think I have a history with them," explained Eddy. "So here's what I'd like to know. Do the black-and-white pockets, these dimensions, if you will, have any sort of connection?"

"I've been waiting for you to ask that, Eddy. Turns out, they do. But I'd be uber careful, as our molecules would not like skipping dimensions rapidly. I'd say, if you need to 'jump,' max it out at two uses. Three if you're in danger, and four if you need to make a sacrifice play, because that is what it'll come to," advised Marshall.

"Then let's choose only one destination, the only one we need, really. The house of Macht. It is in the Castle *des Fluss* in Eastern Europe," said Eddy. Everyone paused and simultaneously looked up at Eddy.

"How, how do you know this?" asked Marshall with expressed horror on his face.

"My memory chip told me when I used it with the staff. It's complicated."

"I don't think so, Eddy. I think there's something you're not telling us. The only way for you to have knowledge like that, using a device like that, is if you two somehow share a similar consciousness or memory…." the ratiocinator specialist trailed off in his point.

"What are you not letting us know, Eddy?" he asked. Eddy lowered his head in overwhelming shame and guilt. Following a moment of introspection and coping, Eddy spoke, for a heavy conscience can only be heavy and hold its burden so long. When the foundation can no longer hold its walls of corruption, the house reduces to rubble. A sandstorm of sorrow can only follow.

"Macht is my clone. I created him. There you have it. You're all here because I, Edward Malcolm, screwed up big time. He was supposed to be my lab assistant. He was—"

"Tell us the truth, Eddy!" demanded Marshall. Eddy cried in bitter remorse.

"H-he was made to be my war replacement because I was a coward!" tears flowed down Eddy's face.

"That's all we needed. You were indeed the Baron Rogue all this time?" asked the brigade. Eddy sort of nodded.

"This was never what I had in mind. I lost myself in this mess," Eddy said.

"You did what every sane man would've done. Running from war, seeking a path to life. If all Macht knows is war, then he simply can't see victory through the side you took, Eddy. Do you know what that means to your people?" asked Marshall.

"Betrayal. Denial. Whatever, just name it. Call it out like the failure it is. It can't mean anything else but that," cried Eddy.

"Probably. But here's what I'm seeing, Eddy. As far as we know, Macht is out there planning the end of us all. We will go after him together. You have our support, Captain Malcolm," assured Marshall, getting nods from the rest of the brigade. "It is only this way that hope is possible. What is hope, if not the endeavors of those that try, and try together no less?"

"I guess this is it then. My last chance at redemption. It's all or nothing. I really don't want to do it, but I need to. I will be free at last," said Eddy.

"This all explains why these gaps in reality are your unpatched or 'struggle' memories. Before we go, I have one last question," asked Marshall. "You are the Baron Rogue that Rebekah and Kathryn talked about, aren't you?" asked Marshall with a smile. Eddy smirks and thinks for a second. He fumbles and shakes his head 'yes' in a gradually firm way.

"Thought so," said Marshall. "Let's go finish this mission, Eddy. Together!" cried Marshall. The brigade raise their weapons to the sky and chant in unison while pumping their weapon arms.

"Where should we drop in? I imagine his level of security is unfathomable. Or dangerously inadequate to the uneducated observer. No in between," said Marshall.

"Check the map for a point outside the walls. If we land far enough outside his radar, we can 'island hop' from point to point until we reach the main gate. We have two problems, however. First, we will need enough power to execute the joints, and we'll need to know how many precisely. Second, where do we find an army large enough to take down the largest threat to ever exist?"

"Heheheh, oh Eddy, do I have a question for you! Where do you get such little faith? Did you think you were the only one with scientific tricks of his own?" taunted Marshall. He and the brigade pressed a button on their armor that gave them the same style and cloaking which Eddy witnessed back at Zero Naught.

"That was you guys?! Wait, that makes sense, actually. Lemme guess…." said Eddy.

"Yep! Courtesy of Lieutenant Kathryn! Isn't she just fiercely fantastic?" appraised Marshall.

"You're absolutely right. Men, time to prepare for the mightiest triumph of our lives. For Kathryn and Rebekah! For all humanity!" rallied Eddy.

"But first, we need you to try the modified version of The Warden's weapon. It should be fully integrated with your memory chip now. That is, you can do as you please with it. Go try it out on a couple of pockets! Someone grab a pen and paper so we can write this down," said Marshall.

"Does this new weapon have a name?" Eddy asked.

"Lightfall. It is the binding-up of all darkness, the song of the exiled," answered Marshall.

Outside the lab, Eddy used Lightfall to locate a nearby dimensional pocket. The team watched from a distance. He found one near a destroyed automobile. When he neared it, he stuck out his weapon. A slow wave of electrical energy wobbled up the staff. Eddy took a step of faith forward.

Inside this pocket, he could not see his team, and the environment around him was completely dissimilar from its parallel in every aspect of the word. The demolished car was restored. The laboratory was in full glory, not a sign of a patch or scratch anywhere in sight.

Above him shone the daystar upon his bewildered brow. Each plant on the ground tossed easily in the leisurely breeze. A minute of gracefulness had Eddy questioning his place in the infinitely finite universe, as most opportunities like these do. He stepped out from the blissful scene and back into this reality.

"Well, Eddy, what'dya see in there?!" they asked.

"Everything. I saw the peace this world has to offer. What happened? Where was I?"

"You either went 7 years forward or backward in time. That is what I found from studying the pockets. It really varies one from the next, and there is no telling which direction you go. You must be prepared for whatever you will see, which is anything. Do not be alarmed at any horrors you might see."

"What do you mean?" asked Eddy.

"Step into another pocket and find out exactly what I mean…." said Marshall.

Again, Eddy used Lightfall to find another pocket to discover. Over there, by the mailbox, yes! It's right there! One foot at a time, so curiously paced. In this dimension, Eddy saw a scene so regrettable it filled his stomach to the brim with disgust. The once euphoric area was now engulfed in flames, the laboratory demolished, nothing left but a crumbling cornerstone. He could hear a voice cry for help, the sounds of footsteps running closer and closer.

Behind him it sounded like Macht himself was talking, saying something near-incomprehensible:

"Run, run… You cannot run. Free yourselves, you cannot. Everything will BURN!"

Eddy's heart rate soared instantly. He raced out of this dimension, stumbling to do so. Upon exiting, he was on the ground, panting for a chance at another breath, his heartbeat almost audible. The team crowds around him.

"Wanna talk about it?" they asked.

"No…. I wish to never speak of these images. What if I can't do this after all? What if… What if I… I-I'm not, I'm not enough….?" replied Eddy.

Marshall, by himself, laughed so vivaciously that it reverberated off all his surroundings. Eddy returned a look of rejection and dissatisfaction. After Marshall quieted down, he kneeled beside Eddy and said in a voice so tender and soft, one could have mistaken it for silk:

"You're not the first soldier to think that. But we're here to accomplish great things, and so are you. Now get up, and come with us. Destiny awaits." They helped Eddy up by the arms and hands.

"I'm ready," said Eddy, catching his breath. "I think it's time to fight back."

Familiar footsteps echoed through the four walls of Zero Naught. The person went straight for the storage room computer, put on a headset, tinkered with the frequencies on an externally-connected radio, and broadcasted for a response.

"Hey, Jorax, wake up! Come on, you gotta get up!" called the voice.

"W-who said that? How'd you get inside my mind?"

"Jorax, Eddy needs us, it's time to go!"

"Is that really you? It is finally time? I-I will get ready and meet you at once!" The person quickly spun the frequency dial to the next name on the list.

"Warden, are you there? It's me," asked the voice.

"I am here, and I am free. You are coming in rather loud and clear," answered the Warden.

"Listen up, Eddy's in trouble and he needs us. We have to move and fast!"

"I will be there straightway, you can count on it!" replied the Warden. The person carelessly trashed the headset and stuffed an empty two potato sacks with various ammunition and modified weapons and left the building.

CHAPTER XVI

WITH TWAIN THEY DID SPEAK

Back at Castle *des Fluss*, Macht is well ahead into preparing his own army. Is this arsenal appropriate? Arguably. For someone to have no stated fear of the oncoming conflict, a great deal is being shown. Absurd, or perhaps pertinent?

Okami presents Macht's war armor to him.

"As requested, a suit of armor capable of harnessing interdimensional energies and various other aberrant vitalities," said Okami. Macht humbly accepted and commended Okami's excellent craftsmanship.

"Most appreciated, brother. Those who deny true power are doomed to bear humility against their own will. And I will make sure he knows it all," said Macht with a voice of sinisterly stern audacity.

On the top right of the chestpiece, the numbers "317" are engraved. On the top left of it, "0116" is engraved as well. For what is the meaning of these numbers? Macht believes they hold the key to unity. To erase all the damage that Eddy has done,

Macht cannot be convinced otherwise that resetting the minds, and even lives, of the entire planet is the only way to accomplish this goal.

History: rewritten. Science: revised. Art: reframed. The precise exodus of the current era will be completed once Macht assumes full control of the Baron Rogue. The only hope is the memory chip. If Eddy is able to restore it to its former glory, Macht cannot win. If he succumbs to the easy temptation of failure, then all hope, all dreams even, are no more.

Macht steps out onto the balcony of the upper floor of his castle. In his stony courtyard below, he peers upon all his subjects. To Macht's right is Okami. To his left is a newly elected guardian, honing the title of Defensor Supremus. Across the top right of his armor reads the label "кара," and the translation of which was written below the label, meaning, "Retribution." The price for condemnation is an indignant wage set forth by the persecuted.

"Citizens of my land, hear me. Today, I have just one expectation from all of you. Those of you who desire freedom, hone your will and stick to it. The Baron Rogue will be coming to us very soon. And on this day we will make him our captive, then finally, brethren, we will attain unity eternal!" exclaimed Macht. The crowd emerged into a tumult of cheer and battlecry.

Macht turns to his left to ask Retribution a question:

"Are you ready to redeem yourself?" The soldier of valor performed an affirmative half-bow. "I sense they are almost here. Why not greet our guests for us?" The soldier departed at once from Macht's presence.

"What will we do?" Okami asked while they headed back inside the throne room.

"I am finally getting what I have wanted for so long. We will await the Baron Rogue's presence." Macht glanced at the screen with the number "512" on it and stared indefinitely, his face grimacing and squirming with rage.

Each member of the 317 brigade is doing last-minute adjustments to uniforms, weapons, belts, and every nook-and-cranny of his own person. They are standing in a circle formation. Marshall has a remotely operated gadget made specifically for this mission. It rests like a small gauntlet on his wrist. On it is an array of buttons and meters. A single screen gives a digital reading of their destination. According to the shared link between Eddy and Macht, the reading yields somewhere in Germany. How certain. Certainly uncertain, that is.

"Commencing genomic transfer! Hold on, team!" Marshall tapped some buttons on his gadget. "Finalizing transfer in 3. 2. ONE!!" announced Marshall. The landscape flashes an intense white. No more than a brief second later, color swirls into existence once again.

The team appeared under a spreading black poplar tree by the water. That is, the waters which belong to none other than the River Rhine. These banks are on the outskirts of your typical riparian forest.

Next to the tree is an oaken double sign. The bottom sign reads the following:

"South: to Mannheim - That Which Remains," for it did not see more than a charcoal haze for too many a day.

The top sign read this warning:

"North: to Worms - That Which is Above All," for this is the location of Macht's castle.

At horizon's end to the north, the silhouette of the Castle can be seen, lurking as dark as a necromantic icon. This is most appropriate for the consideration of unearthly transactions that have happened there. Strange to all, but it is anyone's wonder as to the meticulous elements.

"So where did we land?" asked a team member.

"Judging from this sign, and what looms in the distance, I'd say about two klicks from our destination," answered Eddy. Another team member passed by the sign and read it.

"Worms… I heard about what happened there. But with Macht's hand on that city, may God help us all," said he. "We march onward and forward. No more let down, no more heartache. We push 'til the last one standing!"

The journey to the outskirts of Worms was a sight of both war-torn villages and flourishing communities on either side of the Rhine. The trouble and grief that anticipates their arrival is not to be trifled with, if only they knew. But if anyone knew of oncoming grief, how might perseverance shine through? It is a painful, never-ending endeavor that requires a daily exchange of laying-down for storing-up. Effort is a mindful practice that is the pathway to accomplishment; all the cogitation in the world alone cannot do this. And so, the fragments of self-pity join in a unified chorus of reform.

The walls and structures which lay-out the city of Worms are many and substantially intricate. Here they arrive now at the first bridge, the old box-girder Nibelungenbrücke, which does provide passage across the River Rhein.

The streets are rather empty, but fanfare music can be heard over some sort of broadcasting system.

Where is everyone? Where is the ambient life? The sky reflects the evening time of day: a crisp reddish-orange, with scarce clouds. Somehow, there is fog scattered throughout the city.

Nearer they approached Castle *der Fluss*, but all the more quiet the city appeared to be. No children at the parks, no passers-by on bicycles, no newspaper readers on the street corners. The Battle of the Bulge ended 13 years ago in January 1945. Is there no recovery to show from there? Random, broken wine glasses are littered throughout the streets. Closer investigation shows evidence of Liebfraumilch residue. There are even puddles of it here and there. Over there, too? No, not there. My, how the ranks have plummeted.

With the Castle in full, plain view now, it sounds fitting to take that last step, but what is this? A battalion of Macht's soldiers emerged from the creeping shadows and abandoned stores and seized the 317 brigade by ambush.

Though the Resistance has risen, Eddy could not bear to see his friends suffer for his actions and mistakes. As the battalion tried to tie them up as prisoners, Eddy remembered to activate his Lightfall, sending a singular transverse pulse of energy in an area around him.

To his benefit, his team was fully kneeled on the ground and therefore out of range of the emission. They advanced now to the bridge which connects to the castle. In the middle of the stony bridge, the delineation of a knightly figure can be discerned. One hand held a katzbalger, and the other a mystical-looking partisan.

"Marshall, you and the others go on, I will hold him off!" They darted away to find another method of entry into the castle. Eddy wondered what sort of magical wits await this battle, if it goes in the same manner as his duel with The Warden.

The figure picks up speed towards Eddy, spinning his katzbalger faster and faster.

Eddy unsheathes Lightfall and changes the color of the sphere to royal blue from a switch in the handle, for he has not learned yet how to adapt its mechanisms through his mind. The new grooves in the lance portion are now emitting the same color. The katzbalger clashes with Lightfall. The ground beneath rippled briefly from a negligible magnitude. Eddy's will was not strong enough to do anything more.

A mixed look of despair and confusion flooded Eddy's face. The knight knocked him away with the other hand. With the partisan, he thrusted forward. Eddy rolled to the side then used the lance-end of Lightfall to get back up.

"Eddy Malcolm detected. Must. ELIMINATE!!" growled the knight, proceeding to slash at Eddy. Eddy ducked below the attack and lunged forward to tackle him behind the force of Lightfall, which is glowing yellow now. Despite the attempt, the knight retaliated with a kickback and charged with his partisan lowered and drawn back, ready to jab. Eddy, discombobulated, weakly struck out Lightfall in a pathetic attempt to guard against the melee.

Lightfall reacted to Eddy's state and glowed red. The partisan split apart against the Resistance held out by Eddy.

"What are you, Malcolm?" asked the knight.

"I don't know who I am, only what I must do. I will restore this world and take back everything Macht has stolen from it."

"Only Macht is able to give. He gives and gives some more; I have been given freedom. I am Retribution, your coffin buried deep within the Earth. Say your prayers, and pray you are heard."

Retribution tossed aside the broken partisan handle and tossed the katzbalger into his other hand. With both hands, Eddy firmly clasped Lightfall, which pulsed a breathing green color. Eddy made the first move and used Lightfall against the ground to blast shards of dirt at Retribution. A couple dents were made in the armor. Retribution looked down and shook his head in pity for Eddy.

In retaliation, he swung his katzbalger in a round fashion, creating stand-still vertical circles that produced terrifying levels of energy.

With his other hand, he punched the circles forward at Eddy and jumped toward him. Eddy dodged the circles, whose velocity increased exponentially as they passed him. When they hit the structures behind him, the buildings imploded. Eddy blocked the slash with Lightfall and tried to push Retribution off him.

"You will kneel to true POWER!!" declared Retribution.

"I WILL NEVER BOW TO CORRUPTION!" angrily shouted Eddy. He changed the colors of Lightfall to white and created a repulsion that sent both of them hurling across space in opposite directions. Eddy smashed into a toppled storefront, and

Retribution rolled a number of times over the bridge, clawing it as he tried to stop.

"The more he recognizes he is the Baron Rogue, the stronger he becomes!" thought Retribution to himself. "My only chance now is to cross the dimension and stab him from behind."

But Eddy was already within a few meters distance of him when Retribution looked up to get his bearings.

"Who are you?!" demanded Eddy. "You cannot comprehend what or who I am. You only need to understand that you must DIE!!' cried he, pressing a warp button on a gadget on his wrist. Through a wormhole of sorts, he instantly appeared behind Eddy, ready to strike him down with a blow to the back of the head. Lightfall reacted and created a repulsion barrier, sending him back through the warp.

"I ask of you now, who are you?" asked he.

"I am Eddy Malcolm, and I will bring Macht to his knees!" Retribution grunted and put away the katzbalger. From his backside he withdrew a pistol with "LT-8" labeled on the side. Eddy recognized the branding, knowing well it belonged to one person alone.

"How... how did he get that?!" thought Eddy. Retribution took aim and the pistol lit up with a bright green. Eddy held out Lightfall. The pistol blasted 3 dark green spheres that bent spacetime as they traveled. Eddy could not block them all and the last sphere rapidly spun him around and sent him flying toward Retribution.

Lightfall quickly glowed yellow and stopped the impact, knocking away Retribution.

"You're a stubborn one, Eddy. But not for long," he said, grabbing an IRAG grenade from his side. He tossed the grenade into the air and fired his pistol to accelerate the grenade.

Before it could reach him, Eddy blasted it right back with Lightfall, causing the grenade to detonate. Retribution fell face-flat to the ground. Eddy walked over and turned him over face-up.

He ripped off the helmet, ready to finish the job. But he could not. Victory can bring out the absolute best or worst in a person, but this reveal was rather devastating, to say the least.

"K-Kathryn…? Is it really you?" Eddy cried, heartbroken, letting go of Lightfall. No response. "Kathryn, SPEAK TO ME, PLEASE!!" Eddy soberly dropped to his knees, sobbing over the presumed corpse of his friend and comrade, and delicately holding her head and face, caressing the features as he does with quavery hands.

"E-eddy, where… where am I?" asked Kathryn.

"We are outside Macht's castle. We found it! Victory is so close! But not like this. This… wasn't supposed to happen. How did this mess happen… How did Macht even do it?"

"Eddy, it was my fault. I spied on them and got caught. They brainwashed me, Eddy. A direct commissioning of my person. My mind…. I had no idea who I was, only what I needed to do. To kill you, for some reason." Kathryn coughs a few times, each time more hoarse than the last.

"But the IRAG just now? You're back to normal. There's hope for you! Please Kathryn! I forgive you, you had no idea!"

"Oh, Eddy. I don't know how…I was so set on ending you. Why forgive me?"

"How could I not forgive you? To the end, Kath. We have to press onward."

"Let's go. I'm better now, just gotta get my bearings." Eddy helped Kathryn off the ground.

Meanwhile, The 317 brigade are flanking to the side of the castle, looking for a means of entry.

"Okay, Barrett, Fire!" Marshall commanded. They launched a propelled grenade at the castle wall. Stone clicked down over stone to the ground, creating a short-lived rumbling sensation in the earth.

"We have a front door for a reason, you know," said someone behind them. They all turned around to see that Okami himself had appeared.

"OKAMI!" they collectively gasped.

"I am the wolf that hunts you and haunts you. Will I find you? Always, without a doubt? When? As I feel like doing so. You'll never be comfortable again," said the Wolf. Marshall got out a secret photon cannon and tried blasting away at Okami, but he was unfazed. Or…was he? His person started flickering and flashing for a few seconds before stopping.

"What have you done?" asked Okami, genuinely surprised at this phenomenon.

"You see, we figured out that your usual appearance is just a hologram, but this time I wanted to make sure. Either way, you're real now…For now!"

"You're all coming with me!" said Okami. With both hands, he pressed a button built into his fists. Ethereal, translucent blue chains pierced the earth beneath the team and wrapped them all together into one package. They fell through the warp under them. It sealed back up. Okami created a warp for himself to meet them back in the throne room balcony. In the distance, Okami saw an innumerous militia rushing toward their befallen castle wall.

"That's not ours," said Barrett. The other team members shrugged.

"I know you're not that coordinated," said Okami.

"It's true, yeah," whispered another member.

"So who has the audacity to breach the unbreakable? Just who is that relentless?"

"Let them come, Okami," said Macht, walking into the scene. "They will fall into my plan all the same." Okami nodded affirmatively and left the room to gather a certain artifact from his chambers.

Eddy and Kathryn traveled across the drawbridge and made their way through the castle courtyard. They ascended the staircases and finally reached the doors to the throne room.

"They are probably…definitely expecting us," said Eddy.

"Absolutely," said Kathryn. "So what's the plan?"

"I didn't think I'd get this far, but if I expose Macht directly to my memory chip, or at least to his 'vital signs,' he should be defeated."

"Then let's do this together."

"Together!" They barged open the doors. But it was too late.

"Just in time and on cue, Eddy" started Macht. "Watch with me, now. As I have said many times, I can't wait to see you." The two armies clashed below the balcony area in Macht's grand courtyard. He had wires from the balcony all the way into the ground underneath the court, and a detonator now revealed in his hand.

"This is for an IRAG! He's going to—" exclaimed Marshall. Bang. They heard an ear-crushing blast that came from the courtyard outside.

The explosion stopped the gunfire, but only for a whole three seconds. The gunfire resumed. Friendly fire, crossfire, confused fire. They watch in horror as the field is leveled with bodies.

Only two soldiers are left standing, wondering who will fire first. They wear the same German flag, the same German uniform. They cry as they feel their fingers involuntarily reach for their triggers. The brothers closed their eyes as the bitter cruelty of war took its course and the last sound of hope rang throughout the city of Worms.

Kathryn, Eddy, and the 317 brigade heavily panted in despair and hopelessness. Out of her anger, Kathryn fired an explosive device at the balcony. Macht is caught off-guard and topples to the ground below with the rubble. Over the ledge, a grappling hook was seen and grabbed hold of Eddy by the legs, wrapping around him and taking him down to the courtyard too. Kathryn ran over the team and tried to free them from their mystical prison, but it was to no avail.

"Hold on! I will try to free you!" cried Kathryn.

"I mean, we sort of have been, but we believe in you!" said they. Footsteps treaded into the throne room. It was Okami. After witnessing this feeble attempt unfold, he said, "I consider myself well-controlled. But this… I'm not missing this chance to absolutely annihilate you all from existence. I will enjoy this. You're all alone this time, Lieutenant," mocked Okami.

"No. She's. NOT!!" shouted a voice. Stepping out of the lurking shadows, a person appeared from the doorway.

Kathryn and the 317 brigade showed an expression of jubilee that could have easily been seen on a child's face at Christmastime.

"Ah, General Rebekah. What an unpleasant surprise," taunted Okami.

"I gotta admit, that was a nice trick you played on Eddy back at the hospital, but you'll never get the chance with me, you sheep in wolf's clothing! You're DEAD!!" Rebekah struck a fighting pose, knife and gun in hands. Okami unintentionally winced against his will, but let out a subtle "hmph" to not let it show.

"And let's not forget about the friends she brought along," said two more emerging from the obscurity of the hallway. Jorax and The Warden came bursting through the walls and into the light to assist the resistance against Okami. Their demeanors and appearance looked vastly different than before. Is this truly how freedom feels?

On the ground below, Eddy struggled back to his feet. Macht was nowhere in immediate sight. Looking towards the fallen wall, Eddy saw his figure, dodging and tripping over the perished bodies.

Macht is almost outside the castle walls now—there is no time to be lost. This is it.

Eddy could return home, and let him escape. They could all start over; no one would have to perish or suffer anymore, should the Power that be fulfill the iniquity that is. And how quite a rather significant turpitude it is.

But instead, it came to pass that Eddy dusted himself off with an unprecedented fervor in his spirit and sought after Macht, with all the stonehard determination in this world, as it were.

CHAPTER XVII

AS IT WERE

"Give it up! We have you!" exclaimed Rebekah.

"Not quite, General," retaliated Okami. He pounded his fists together. His armor, even his fur-lined coat, morphed into a clanky suit of tiered steampunk-like armor from shoulder to toe. The outside shoulders were embedded with round niches that housed a fan on either side. A pressure gauge is situated on the upper portion of his right chest. Okami's helmet became a completely metallic gas mask, down to the venting system over the chin area. The glass visor is now continuous from one eye to the other, as opposed to extending from the midface to the top of the head. His new weapon, the Soulsplitter, resembled a gunto ceremonial sword, but with an array of gadgets and a gratuitous amount of bolsterings.

"You, the arrogant, stubborn people you are, have chosen the path of the foolish. Welcome to the end. Allow me to guide you all swiftly to the next path: underground, next to Eddy Malcolm, and six feet under!" howled Okami.

Okami snatched a steam grenade from his side and detonated it onto the ground in front of him. Diverse colors were highlighted throughout the steam. A green fire followed the steam. The four intently surveyed and waited, cautiously navigating each step.

When it cleared, Okami could be seen sinking his right claws into the stone floor. After a brief struggle, he ripped up a chunk and hurled it toward Jorax, sending him rolling a distance despite his attempt to counter-block it.

The Warden leaped forward at Okami, but the fires mutated into acid. Okami blasted away the Warden with a forceful puff of steam, shredding some of his armor from the sheer pressure. Kathryn and Rebekah charged from the flanks, but Okami teleported a short distance ahead using a switch on his wrist.

"A feeble effort," mocked Okami.

In Okami's conceit, Jorax charged at him and rammed him back-first into the wall.

"Nice one!" cried Rebekah.

Okami switched his weapon's setting. He brutally slashed the air in front of him, creating rips in the ambient spacetime. In these rips, gravity is modified to be either ten times greater or less than its earthly value.

Okami bounded up where the gravity was less and densely pummeled his weapon to the floor where gravity was greater, smashing the rest of the floor into many large chunks.

Rebekah drew her pistol and shot at the platform Okami stood on. Okami freely moved to another, for he was in control of the gravity around himself. With his teleporter, he appeared behind Rebekah. As he cocked back his arm to strike her, the

Warden mightily leaped over and blocked the melee. Rebekah turned around and shot Okami's kneecap but to no avail. The armor is nigh impregnable.

From the side, Kathryn tossed up a grenade. Jorax batted it with a great swing toward Okami. Rebekah and the Warden hurdled away, mostly unscathed but not without appreciably rough landings.

Okami's armor absorbed most of the blast's impact, but he was not happy by any dastardly fumes of fantasy itself.

He used Soulsplitter to repair the spacetime ripples, and in its place he imposed a time dilation effect by elegantly swaying his sword, finishing the dance by pulling the sword from right to left at eye level and precisely parallel to the ground.

Jorax attempted another charge at him, but the transition was already done. Okami was now able to move at twice his speed, while everyone else could only move at half their best.

Okami took advantage of this with uttermost prejudice to instill many concussive blows to the Warden and his armor. In a fight against time itself, Kathryn fired LT-8 at Okami to distract him, but his figure only rippled like disturbed pond water.

He ceased the time dilation.

"This next trick is courtesy of Malcolm Zero!" warned Okami.

"How does he even know who that is?" asked Rebekah to herself. Okami copied his weapon into two, thus allowing him to activate full influence over matter, down to the molecular level, transforming it into whatever he desired. He struck a stone column nearby, altering it into a pillar of red flames.

Jorax saw this opportunity to blast his own fire through them toward Okami, but it evaporated into steam upon hitting Okami's weapon, and the steam in turn changed into glass that drifted away like a leaf in the wind.

Jorax could not believe this absurdness. Rebekah waited in the corner to eye any opening. Kathryn and the Warden firmly stood back to back. Warpings were anticipated.

As the battle for reality progressed, Marshall and the 317 were finding a way to break free from their ethereal chains.

Okami propelled his guntos at Jorax using steam power. Before they reached him, Okami teleported in front of Jorax and caught them. He goes for a clean sweep of the chest, but Jorax ripostes him with his own swords.

Okami twirled violently to make a hurricane of steam about himself, knocking everyone away and crashing them into the closest object. Rebekah was struck down and knocked out after being plowed through a stone column.

The Warden unsheathed his hand cannon and blasted a number of rounds at Okami. But he cut them in half with Soulsplitter. One more chance. The Warden tinkered with his final round and adjusted a few switches.

This time, upon firing, the round exploded into an assault of smaller but more concentrated explosions around Okami. Okami, most annoyed now, launched one of his swords into the shoulder of the Warden, pinning him into the wall. Fortunately, in his rage, Okami only pierced the layered armor.

"I have a better idea for you," muttered Okami to himself. He warped over to the Warden and used the blunt end of

Soulsplitter to incapacitate him through a manipulation of his psyche, that is, whatever remained that belonged to Okami after the IRAG reversal.

Kathryn sprinted over to stop this, but Okami, with his free hand, drew his pistol and shot Kathryn with a four-dimensional bullet that traps the victim inside a temporary spacetime pocket. Jorax refused to let his friends ignite his swords and dashed at Okami. The two clanked and brawled. Strike after strike they continued. Their swords crossed in an 'X' fashion.

An ill look of animosity consumed Jorax's face, for Okami had inculcated all those years of trepidation into Jorax.

"You were never enough, and you never will be," whispered Okami to Jorax.

Jorax screamed with all he had and shoved Okami away. Every blow of his fiery swords into Okami's armor lacerated it wide open. His grip was so tense on his weapons that his right sword flung out of his hand and toward the chained-up 317 brigade. He dropped the other sword, unsheathed his mace and pummeled Okami in the stomach with it. Jorax did not hesitate to follow that up with a strong kick. He went for an overhead strike from his mace, but Okami caught it.

"I've... absolutely had it with you, pest!" grunted Okami.

"Men, we need to act, and now!" said Marshall to his fellow brigade. "Sir, we'll die! Look, even Rebekah and all them are almost no match!"

"Don't give me excuses, I know the odds! We can do it! We have to try! Give me that sword, I'll do it myself if I have to! For Rebekah! For the 317! For everyone!"

"Hoo-yah!" chanted the brigade in unison. Marshall used his feet to obtain Jorax's loose sword on the ground. Through careful maneuvering, he transferred it to his hands and sawed the chains and freed himself and the 317 brigade. Okami charged up Soulsplitter and prepared his arm to end Jorax. But the 317 all jumped onto and tackled Okami.

Aside from Jorax's sword, they had no weapons, only fists, guts, and a desire for freedom. Punch after kick they bombarded Okami. He is trying to stand back up, but the repetitive strikes are preventing him.

Rebekah awakened again. She is mustering her strength to get back up to fight. She faintly sees the 317 fighting Okami, who is oddly confused they would even try something so half-witted.

Okami swung his arms and broke free.

The 317 backed off, knowing they were bested, but Marshall went in again alone with Jorax's sword. He crossed with Okami's Soulsplitter.

"You have been the thorn in my flesh. You do not know when to give up. How illogical," said Okami.

"Logic this, you swine!" Marshall whirled Okami's sword away, spun, and slashed Okami's armor in the left shoulder. The sword became stuck there.

To play along, Okami dropped to his knees and pretended to be defeated. Marshall turned his back and walked away, raising his arms in victory at his friends.

The 317 cheered for him, but it was short lived. They began waving their hands in front of themselves to signal to Marshall to watch out behind him.

"MARSHALL!!" shouted Rebekah. Marshall's glee turned into a countenance of regret. Okami motioned his hand forward and stabbed Marshall where he stood. A painful yelp followed.

He removed Soulsplitter and left Marshall. Rebekah and the 317 ran over to receive Marshall's final words.

"M-Marshall?" weeped Rebekah.

"Of all the odds I ever thought of, I could never figure out how you were such a good friend to us, Rebekah," said Marshall, grappling for breath.

"Marshall, no. No, no, don't leave. We need you, I need you!" sobbed Rebekah. Marshall placed his hand on her arm.

"It's going to be okay. Trust me—0116, remember?" said Marshall with his final breath in this world.

Okami watched as Rebekah and the brigade mourned their friend's death. She bawled and poured her tears over the body. Her sadness quickly changed to burning anger.

"How pathetic," said Okami. "And to think you even thought about stopping Macht? Get ahold of yourselv—"

Rebekah grabbed him by the throat.

"You. Are mine alone!" cried Rebekah. Rebekah swings the barrel of her pistol and shoots Soulsplitter, sending them both into a separate dimension.

She held nothing back. She battered and struck him as hard as she could with violent barrages. Okami tried slicing at her, but she intercepted and ripped Soulsplitter out of his hand and kneed him in his solar plexus. She swept Okami's legs and sent him face-up onto the ground. Rebekah grabbed Soulsplitter and used its handle to smash his helmet so she could personally tear his face apart.

The glass of his vizor broke. At last, Rebekah could see his wrathful emerald eyes. She paused for a moment. It wasn't enough. She hacked the helmet into two jagged halves. The sound of the pieces contacting the floor echoed clearly into her ears.

Her anger met a full stop. She recognized that face.

"You... How... Why?! You were dead, I saw it with my own eyes!" exclaimed Rebekah. Okami growled and pressed a button on his wrist that transferred him outside of this dimension. Rebekah is warped back to where she was. Jorax, the Warden, and Kathryn all returned as the effects of Okami wore off with his disappearance.

"He got away? Just like that?" questioned Rebekah, arms abroad.

"Pathetic. He's out there in hiding I am sure. Leave him. We need to find Eddy," said Kathryn.

"We will take Marshall's body back and give him a proper rest. You all go on ahead. I think we've seen enough," said the 317 brigade.

Rebekah and Kathryn exchanged a look then nodded at them, as if to say, "Yes, they have been through more than enough. Let them go."

Macht is limping through the ruins and rubble of the city of Worms. The crimson-tainted sky is polluted with smog from the wake of Rebekah's team. Macht reached for his specialized inter-reality radio at his side.

"Okami, give me a hand, will you?!" said Macht over his radio. It reached Okami in the real world.

"Working on it! The signal is being jammed by a proximal source. Do you have a visual on anything that could be causing that?" asked Okami.

"The only thing that could match the frequency would be..." muttered Macht.

"Macht!!" A voice rang out loud-and-clear. Macht stopped limping. He knew that voice. He turned around. Macht firmly grasped the radio and clenched his teeth.

"Okami. This is it." Static crackle. Macht almost crushed the radio with his tight grip, but he put it back to his side. An eerie feeling stopped him from disposing of it.

"Give it up. We both know you are in no shape to fight me. I am the most powerful being in this reality! You should know." said Macht.

"I fear you no more!" exclaimed Eddy.

"If this hellscape is worth saving to you, I will not hold back from finishing my goal. I am no longer your manifested protocol!" Macht replied. Eddy and Macht walked towards each other until they stood fifty feet apart.

"You have to stop all of this!" said Eddy.

"You don't think I've tried stopping? Guess what: I did, and it didn't work! The pain it caused me, the fiery hell I went through for you, FOR YOU! Tell me, was I your 'Little Boy' or your 'Fat Man'? Your pacifism and intellect—converted to a single entity of absolute emotionless madness. I AM THIS. ALL THANKS TO

YOU. And now, everyone must suffer all because of YOU! I am Macht, for I am POWER!" said Macht.

Macht starts to sprint toward Eddy. Eddy, shaking his head awake, sprints back toward him. Eddy reaches for a disc in his side pocket and actuates the disc. It becomes a dual-bladed shuriken. He hurls the shuriken at Macht. Macht limbos underneath it.

Macht draws a knife from his leg pouch and jabs at Eddy's chest. Eddy blocks it with his foot, the knife drops, and he draws his revolver to shoot Macht. Macht catches the returning shuriken and counters the shot by spinning the blades. He uses the momentum to slice at Eddy, who has unsheathed Jorax's Longsword.

Clang after clang, the two cannot land a direct hit on each other. Eddy managed to get the blade into the center of the disc, disarming Macht. Macht spun to elbow Eddy's jaw; Eddy hindered the force with the side of his forearm. He returns the blade to its sheath.

Eddy roundhouse kicks Macht; he catches Eddy's foot and throws him down to go for a punch to the face. Eddy grabs the knife on the ground. His right hand swipes at Macht's face. Macht clasps Eddy's fist with his left hand to pry away the attack, but Eddy uses his other hand to throw Macht off him while turning his own body. Macht rolls back up as does Eddy.

"You are a stubborn fool!" said Macht.

"I'll take it to your grave!" mocked Eddy. "This is my world, where I do as I please!" Macht stretched out his hand and dimensional pockets appeared randomly all around. Who knows what all is hidden in those?

"You know, Macht, I faced a lot of doubt and denial trying to find you. But I learned something along the way. This entire place, this world. It was—and is—my reality. And that's why I'm going to defeat you. You designed it for my downfall, but I used it to build an empire of freedom. Once I came to terms with who I truly am, I have never been more content."

Furious and hellbent, Macht raises his left arm. A chunk of the rubble forms into a sphere. Macht spins it and uses his right hand to blast it toward Eddy. Eddy jumps to his right but the mass hits his left shoulder.

"AGH!!" cried Eddy. There is an open abrasion there left from the trajectory.

"This is my reality, Eddy. Get used to it!" bellowed Macht.

Eddy, realizing no other option, launched himself fist-first into Macht by way of Lightfall. Macht blocked the melee with his right forearm, reinforced by assimilated rubble. He created an energy-formed barrier that ejected Eddy backward a great distance into the earth.

Eddy dropped Lightfall in the midst of it. Macht picked up Lightfall with his left hand. Eddy is crouching on the ground. Macht warps the terrain underneath Eddy and uses it to propel Eddy towards him, smashing Eddy through the various pocket dimensions during his flight. The sphere end of Lightfall is pointing out toward Eddy. Macht turned the sphere's color to a violently dark red and hurled Eddy back into the ground.

"You were too late, Eddy. All the world. Lost. But not I. To be an exception, you must accept what is. And I changed it to its full potential, under my foot and in my clutch. Surely, destiny dances with delight. She tells me, 'I am home.' And I reply, simply, 'Welcome back'."

Macht twirled around Lightfall to its lance end, preparing to finish Eddy, who is weakly holding onto himself. His vision is blurry, fading in and out. Eddy could hear the cries of those who loved him.

"EDDY!!' cried Rebekah, running to help, but Kathryn, Jorax, and the Warden were holding her back with all they had.

"He must do this on his own!" they explained, weeping.

"Eddy, I believe you can do this! YOU CAN WIN!" She fell to her knees. For one steady moment in his life, Eddy cast away all the thoughts in his mind to focus on what needed to be done. He could see Lightfall pointed straight at him.

"No. It's not going to end this way again." Eddy coughed and groaned. "I am the BARON ROGUE!" Lightfall glowed intensely, the memory chip separating from it and telekinetically fusing into Eddy.

He stood up and knocked Macht down, reclaiming Lightfall from him. Eddy's body radiated with a shining brilliance. His shoulder healed as well. This is the Baron Rogue Proper in his true form. There is no scar deep enough to stop him.

"We need to get far away!" exclaimed Kathryn. They fled back to the castle outskirts just across the bridge.

A blue cape formed about Eddy's backside, his armor repaired. Lightfall copied itself in two and briskly pulled into Eddy's hands, royal blue sparks flying around his wrists. His entire eyes gleamed with a blinding white color for an entire half-minute. Macht, half-sitting up on the ground, vividly beheld the image of the Baron Rogue Proper, causing him to wince and cover his own eyes with a hand during the transformation.

"I'm taking back everything!" shouted Eddy. Eddy clasped together the two weapons and turned the entire battlefield to the gray pocket dimensions to disable any further tricks from Macht. They were able to see each other clearly. Without another word, Eddy charged at Macht with help from the two Lightfalls propelling him forward. Several pocket dimensions split apart, restoring their colors.

Through each one, Eddy kept his eyes off the unspeakable horrors that dwelled, no matter how horrible and wretched. His focus was sure. Penetrating from the last dimension, Eddy kicked Macht in his chest, blasting him a great distance.

Macht pushed himself up to shoot his guns, but Eddy was not in sight. Knife in hand, but it is of no use in a war of sticks and stones. Eddy emerged from the dimension behind Macht and shoved him into another with his arms.

In this dimension, there is luscious greenery all around. Wild colors paint the flora here. Macht was on guard, nonetheless. Eddy appeared before him in an instant and pounded the ground with both spheres, rippling and shattering this world into an untold amount of colossal airborne fragments. Macht tried leaping across the pieces to get himself to Eddy, but Eddy spun and flung each one outward into nothingness.

Macht found himself freefalling, but he was soon interrupted by breaking through another dimension and landing on fire-hot coals. In this world, the previous scene was reduced to ashes. Macht could not see, for the smoke was too intense. Harsh coughing and wheezing filled every second, seemingly crushing his windpipe.

A hundred versions of Eddy appeared as the fragments from before. This scene combined with the smoke rendered it difficult to make out where he was. Macht looked all around to no avail, his heart rapidly pounding by the second. Eddy sprung up from beneath and grabbed Macht by his foot, and used the Lightfall in his other hand to blast him through many more pocket dimensions.

Eddy broke both Lightfalls with his hands, causing the grayed-out battlefield to return to its former obscurities. Eddy ripped out the memory chip from himself and activated it. The entire battlefield swirled like a whirlpool, converging onto him. Macht tried to escape but could not successfully fight against the heavy earthen waves. He turned to face Eddy and tried shooting at him, but the bullets disintegrated every time. Eddy firmly snapped his fingers on his left hand and the madness stopped. Macht is half-kneeling, trying to catch his breath.

They are face-to-face now.

"You don't have the will to do it!" taunted Macht, on his last string of hope to consume Eddy.

"My will is incomputable; it's over," said Eddy. He forcefully planted the memory chip into Macht's forehead.

"O-Okami, wake this punk up!" cried Macht.

"What?!" exclaimed Eddy.

CHAPTER XVIII

THE SIN'S VITAL SIGN

For a man that avoided his wars, perhaps how cowardice, that he was also the greatest patriot that ever lived.

From dust to dust, the current world disappeared, and Eddy found himself back at the lab underneath the office building, the same in which Macht induced him into his mental battlefield. They must have ended the simulation to make their escape with what they had. Eddy was presumably alone in the room, but there was a door open to his left. In the mirror, he sees that he has de-aged, the same as he was back in the previous world. Is this a temporary effect?

Eddy felt some kind of object at his side. Fumbling in his coat pocket, he found…his memory chip?! He placed it back in there for safe-keeping. He grabbed a gun off the wall and attached it to his side. Next to his chair was a pedestal for an artifact entitled "the memory collection and storage of the Baron Rogue Proper". It was empty, of course. Eddy pursued down the hallway after Macht and Okami.

In the southern-most recesses of this same room, Okami could actually be found perusing file after file, upon realization of what Eddy had found in the office during the simulation.

"My father's last known location was Paris? That cannot be right. No, that can't be right! He was home! Father, WHY?!" cried Okami.

He found the folder with the wrinkled paper detailing his father's whereabouts. Closer inspection revealed a faded line stating the date of his father's death: August 6, 1945. Okami released his grip on the folder. That was the same day he had dropped the stolen atomic bomb on Paris. Every bit of knowledge, all his intellectual assets, meant nothing anymore. The only people he loved were consumed by the very fire he had created.

"All those years I would write to them with no response back. I thought I was no longer wanted, that they had ceased to be proud of me and my life's work and highest aspirations. No, I will not go down this way. I have one last chance to restore myself.

"I cannot undo my evils, but I can still do something. Macht... That manipulative, conniving creature! He must be DESTROYED!" Okami inserted a neuronal bullet into his handgun, which was labeled "LT-8" for personal convention, and proceeded down the hallway as well.

At the end of the hallway, Eddy stumbled into a circular room, with a cathedral-like ceiling. Macht stands on the opposite side, pointing his own handgun directly at Eddy. Eddy gasped with heavy exasperation.

"Listen to me carefully, as your life depends on it," said Macht. Eddy started scanning the room for any element he could use in this situation, however unique as most of his situations are. To Eddy's left, on the wall, is a screen mounted in this room. It is displaying Macht's and Okami's names with a number underneath each name. That is, these numbers are also their vital signs, if you will. An error sign is visible with a countdown timer going as well, stating that Macht needs to complete a charge or it will all shut down.

At the rate the timer is going, it will not be long. But why did Macht have to go through all that trouble instead of killing Eddy? Oh, he knew that killing Eddy would eliminate the memory and, thus, himself. He needs it, but Eddy has to be alive. But the others were induced by IRAGs, so why not Eddy? It is for this reason, Macht deduced, that Eddy was nigh immune because of the source interference.

Eddy stalled a moment to talk to Macht. Each prolonged moment was another drive into the spikes for Macht's grave.

"Why did you come back?" Macht asked, on the verge of a breakdown, but his facades were strong.

"I couldn't let this happen. This wasn't supposed to be how things turned out."

"Oh, but it did! Isn't it beautiful? I am in command! This earth is mine as I envision it! I sit on my throne—and the world beneath me slaves at my will. It is, simply, perfect."

"The kingdom shall fall, Macht. You were never the king," said Eddy.

"Is that so, Eddy? Did you finally get what you wanted?" asked Macht, lowering his gun.

"I never got what I wanted, and I've been paying the price all these years," replied Eddy.

"So the truth comes out finally... You're too late, old friend. Oh, all the hell-fire and brimstone that I went through for you. And for what? More recognition for Eddy Malcolm?

"I tore apart reality before your eyes, Eddy. And I sat back and laughed hysterically as society purged itself. No one recognized anyone anymore, and it was glorious. Who is friend? Who is foe? Fame has no place if it gets you killed. You're a wanted criminal, and all you did was walk out your front door. That's exactly what I went through for you. FOR YOU!! "I loved every day of the purge. And you want to know why? Everyone was able to experience a mere glimpse of my daily, agonizing pain. And so, mine was relieved."

"I recognize that no amount of apologies will make what I did right, but I can still save you with the memory chip. I can give you hope! You can live the life you could never have but always wanted!" pleaded Eddy. Macht did not have to take any time to think about this proposition. His mind was too set on his goal.

"You would like that scape-goat of a catharsis, wouldn't you? No more experiments, Eddy! I was achieving global unity! I stopped the war! And all it took was another one in the right place—in your mind, battle after battle. I have rewritten history with my own hand! But what shall I be remembered for, Eddy? Tell me!"

"You are the version of me I never truly wanted. Out of my fear alone you were created. But instead of the world's greatest ally, you became humanity's worst enemy. Entirely my fault? Yes, but for what? I guess it takes more than an IQ of 512 to figure that out, huh?" Eddy gestured to the screen. "Just as I once did, you relied too much on your intellect, and now you're scraping for any level of understanding. Yet we're finding nothing, are we? We will go down in history, no doubt, as the most dissatisfied men to have ever lived. Make sure you write that down."

"Your words were always aimed for motion. Some sparks will never ignite the flame. For someone who loved to gamble, you struggled to beat the odds. But I just hope, this time, you have the right cards." Macht pressed a button on the console and showed him Rebekah in an incapacitated state.

"Rebekah!! Don't you worry, I'll get you out of this!" cried Eddy.

"You'll never save her without your precious memory chip completed," said Macht.

Okami surged ferociously into the room, almost breathless. He pointed his gun at Macht. Without another word, he shot Macht with the neuronal bullet, causing brief shock by expropriating the nervous system, as it were. Okami, not thoroughly transmuted by power like Macht, had comparably dignified qualities, as if Macht had a choice in the low-stakes matter. However it may be, the truth be revealed that Macht had never told Okami about his parents' death in Paris.

"Brother? What is this?" asked Macht, groaning from twinging pain.

"Why were my parents in Paris?!" yelled Okami angrily.

"Okami?! What are you talking about!" defended Macht.

"You cursed fool! They were in Paris when I bombed it!! YOU KNEW THIS! What are you hiding from me?!" shouted Okami.

"H-how did you learn this?" Macht asked.

"I paid a visit to my file which Eddy stumbled upon in the office during his simulation. It looks like you didn't rewrite all parts of history. You were afraid of something! What was my father building, Macht?" demanded Okami.

"What do they even mean in the vast plot of it all? Our focus was clear, our goal realized!" exclaimed Macht. Okami sneered angrily, ready to end him.

"Knowing who my father and his father before were, I'd say they were building some friendly competition, which, as we all know, none of us here like. Oh, the truth is always found out," Eddy said. "I know this more than any. And the things I learned on the battlefield that you created, Macht—quite deadly."

"Eddy, I could never repay you, but at the same time I've never wanted you so dead," Okami assured.

"Quite understandable," agreed Eddy.

"The both of you... against me. My own, and my brother. I truly am alone. I'll have the honor of engraving both your tombstones. Don't worry, I'll make it memorable. The world will know your betrayals." said Macht.

"Enough!" Eddy enacted.

He removed his memory chip from his pocket and inserted it into the central console to sabotage Macht's life system, after hopes of urging Macht had been extinguished. Macht dropped his handgun, but he could not react quickly enough to reverse the chip. His muscles tensed up with an apparent tetany. He is nearly unable to move. The screen began to glitch then showed Macht as a young soldier.

"Private Malcolm reporting for duty!" said young Macht. The scenes jumped around like random pieces of film stuck together for replay. Okami and Eddy watched intently.

"Private! You are a disgrace to the service! Maybe if you put down your journal and pen every once in a while, you'd be a better shot! Disqualified and dismissed!!"

"Give me a chance!" said young Macht.

"That's an order!!" shouted the Sergeant. The scene faded and scrambled into nothingness, like most of Macht's moments in his questionable existence.

"You see now Eddy? We were never meant for this. But look at us now. Who was right? Was it I? Was it you?" said Macht, as honest as a war-torn soul could ever be.

The scene on the screen changed again.

"Captain, the planes with the bombs!" cried a watchman.

"What is it you said?!" asked the Captain.

"They're gone!!" said the watchman.

"They are—WHAT?!"

The screen transitioned to the original interface.

"I saw a vision to get their attention. So prideful they were. I wanted to bring them a humbling experience. I was going to be the Baron Rogue. I am peace. I am power! I am balance! I am—" said Macht in a gradually softening tone.

A number appeared on the screen. It began to count down from 512. That is, Macht's life force.

512.

508.

500.

"Okami... what is this?" Eddy asked.

495.

480.

"This machine is his IQ regulator. Without it, he will destabilize and every particle in his body will become disassembled. Because we never completed our version of your memory chip, when that number reaches zero, he will cease to exist." explained Okami.

460.

430.

410.

"There's no way to stop it, huh?" asked Eddy. Macht is silent, looking steadily back and forth from Okami and Eddy. Okami chuckled once or twice.

"Afraid not," he said. His serendipity faded. "That means I will cease to exist as well. Regrettably, we combined our intellects as one, per our plans for unity." For the first time since before the years of the resistance, Okami removed his helmet ever so hesitantly.

His face was finally revealed, as the sacred identity of the Wolf will no longer be a necessity for too much longer.

Eddy glanced over and was almost too surprised to speak. "Yakeru? I-is that really you?" asked Eddy.

"Hmph. How unfortunate we meet again like this," said Yakeru.

"How did I ever get you involved in this chaos? Jiro would be greatly ashamed of how we perverted engineering like this," said Eddy.

380.

370.

Seek immediate remedy.

Macht fell uncontrollably to one knee, the particles of his being began to fade.

"Eddy, I've always wondered what it would've been like to have celebrated Christmas with you." Macht said weakly, his voice trembling as one coping with overwhelming grief. Truly, that was the scenario. His thought pattern was now disarranged and steadily clambering into unhindered psychoses.

Any distraction was anesthetic medicine.

Eddy only stood there, first emotionless, but the facade did not last long as the tears broke through the axiomatic dam, as reinforced as it were. The walls were torn down at long last.

340.

310.

"I wonder if my homeland would've been proud of my achievements. But what is all that now?" Yakeru said, regretfully. Eddy can only sit down in abeyance and observe everything unfold now. In his mind's eye, he was beginning to accept his personal liability for this entropy.

"Yakeru, what do you want to be remembered for?" asked Eddy, hoping to give any kind of emotional rest to him.

290.

270.

You are approaching critical condition.

"There was nothing I-I did that was worth remembering," said Yakeru, his voice breaking. "Let them know how much of a fool I was, let them know this isn't the way."

Yakeru's molecules began disassembling faster than Macht's. Eddy didn't know what to say. What is there to say to your once-worst enemy, the plaguer of your dreams? Without any notice, none of that mattered anymore. Maybe Macht could still achieve unity after all.

"You know, Eddy, had I seen the light sooner, we could've been great teammates. They would've been proud of us," said Yakeru.

250.

230.

"Goodbye, Eddy," Yakeru said with his last breath, before being completely fading out of reality.

200.

180.

Rebekah is not awake yet; her trance is lifting. It is only Eddy and Macht now that remain in this room. Eddy stepped over to him and kneeled beside him.

"Eddy," said Macht, "why... Why did you create me? I don't understand. I never did. Life—I could never figure it out. I needed help, Eddy. I NEEDED YOU!" grunted Macht painfully.

150.

130.

Systems will not recover.

Eddy's too choked up. He is remorseful over a lifetime of mistakes. If only he had realized sooner that mistakes make the man.

110.

90.

Now, Macht's molecular integrity started being ripped apart and dethreaded.

"So, this must be death. What a terrible fate. He is patient to have waited so long to get me. I deserved it too long ago.

"Now I see it. I see my life. And I hate what I see." Macht closes his eyes. He cannot bear to see the inevitable happen from his own creation.

70.

50.

Failure to thrive.

Shutting down all systems.

The screen fades to red. Macht begins to cry uncontrollably. A great deal of pain sets in; his departure is slower than Yakeru's. He turns his head to Rebekah, who is faintly awake now.

He remembers her kindness to him back at Zero Naught. Is that a smile upon his face? Yes, it is. A second later, he then turned back to Eddy.

"If you don't tell her what you're supposed to, you've wasted your whole life. We'll both have died in vain. Not everyone gets two lives to say 'I love you,' and how foolish it would be to not have used either chance. But it was never my job. Believe me, I wanted to."

40.

30.

20.

"At least you were bold enough to finally be the hero this world needed..." whispered Macht.

15.

6.

Beginning final countdown.

"Macht," said Eddy tenderly.

"What could you possibly want from me?" asked Macht defeatedly.

"I'm sorry, for everything," Eddy weeped bitterly.

"To forgive you... With my last breath? Hm. I am finally at rest." Macht pauses a second to think over it all.

"So long, Eddy. My first friend." A single teardrop runs down Macht's face.

3.

2.

1.

Zero Naught.

Macht's existence dissipated into nothingness. Eddy feels a sudden pain in his chest, and breathing has become increasingly harder.

Rebekah jolts awake and sees Eddy. She looks around and sees the memory chip Eddy inserted into the console and ejects it.

"Eddy, what's this? What's going on? D-did we win?" She asked.

"It is my memory chip. We won, but we have a new problem now that I should've seen coming," replied Eddy.

"Isn't your memory chip everything you've ever known? Isn't that what you need to get back the lost memories? So you could finally find out who you are, before the attack happened?" asked Rebekah.

"It's okay. I am at peace about it. No more room for bitterness. Take it, I want you to have it," insisted Eddy confidently. His breathing hastens as the systemic pain increases. Numbness and pin-like tingling flood over his arms, legs, abdomen, and tongue.

"But why?" Kathryn's voice chimes in from the distance. She heard about what had happened and rushed over. Eddy uses the last of his strength to look at her then back at Rebekah.

"I wanted to replace everything with my memories of you, Rebekah. So when I'm gone, you'll always be here. I love you so much." Eddy pauses a second. "It would have been everything I've ever done right, my Rebekah: loving you."

"EDDY!!" cried Rebekah. "I love you, but we both know life doesn't work like that. Your victory here will be forever remembered now."

"Look at us, reunited at last," said Eddy, as Kathryn came closer.

"Shut up! We never wanted it like this. Eddy, my darling—" cried Rebekah.

"Rebekah, Kathryn. Please tell them. All must know the truth. I was—I am—the Baron Rogue.

"Goodbye, friends. Goodbye, my love." Eddy said with his final breath.

He collapsed to the floor, upon the same spot where Macht once lay. Rebekah and Kathryn pick up the body of Edward J. Malcolm and carry him out on a stretcher onto the ambulance that Kathryn drove over here. They took his body to the hospital.

There, the two of them took the memory chip back to Kathryn's lab, after transferring Eddy's body to be examined for autopsy. No words, only understanding.

Rebekah sits in this special chair that has a brainwave helmet, much similar to the one Eddy sat in for Macht. Kathryn takes a deep breath, her hands somewhat shaky, and inserts the memory chip into her machine.

"Rebekah?" Kathryn said.

"Mhm?" she asked, unsteady as well.

"Whatever you see, just know that I love you. I hope you find what you're looking for." said Kathryn Rebekah nods.

"I'm... I'm ready," she said. Kathryn flips switches, turns gauges, and adjusts some sliders. She watches as Rebekah slips into a dream.

As a dreamer is, so shall they do. It is no mere flip of the coin, such as any chance may be, but rather a conscious application of passion and resolution. This unstoppable force meets a road waiting to be paved only by those daring enough to lay its tedious bricks.

And when the foundation is... So shall there be.

In this <u>beautiful world</u>, Rebekah is in a meadow.

Wildflowers are scattered, with hues of scarlet, goldenrod, and turquoise. The sky is nigh cloudless, a deep blue as rich as the ocean that it would be envious of it all. In the distance, mountains huddle tightly and paint a grandeur-esque skyline. The running of the streams completes the scene marvelously.

Wind gently breezes, and leaves rustle hushedly to add to the ambiance. Sunshine, purest sunshine, makes it warm enough to enjoy it all in carefree bliss. There is a single tree nearby. Its leaves are as green as emerald, and it stands as tall as a two-story building.

As Rebekah looks all around her, she sees that she is alone. She glances down—she is wearing an elegant white skirt that reaches just above her ankles, so that it sways gracefully in the easy-going waves of the wind. A small, round silver pendant is worn about her neck, with the initials "RB" engraved in it. Her blouse is a lighter teal, with shingled ruffles on its sleeves. When she peers at her shadow, and angles herself, there appears to be a sunhat on it. She feels her head, and, oh yes—there is a sunhat, indeed! Euphoria—it feels like a dream, the sweetest fantasy. Ah, she closes her eyes, she cannot believe it. She opens them.

There appears Eddy underneath the single tree. He is leaning his back against it, arms and feet crossed. He seems relaxed, as one who is at peace with himself. Oh, Rebekah runs! And she runs! They embrace like the fondest lovers. Oh, because they are! There are no others to interfere, no one else to break them down. Here, they stand together, as one, just them.

"Eddy, where are we?" asked Rebekah. Only a smile. He tenderly takes her by the hand.

"My dear, we are home," he replied.

"Rebekah, I have one last thing to give you before I depart. I want you to have every last bit of love I ever had, to add to your very own, if it were possible" he said, in reference to what he had left on his memory chip, including this scene for her to explore freely.

"Oh, darling! I am flattered, but I do not desire that. I have all I need already," said Rebekah. Eddy glances down at the pendant and back to her eyes.

"That is wonderful to hear, because it was in you all along; that is, you would've never needed mine, Miss ReBekah—I mean, Miss Rogue Baron."

"I know, my dear, but how magnificent a quality it became!" She grins like one that is guilty from a revealed truth, but a truth that instead adds quality rather than shame. Eddy steps forward from the tree and shows Rebekah his masterpiece he carved into it. Not a single word exchanged, only appreciation of a moment suspended in time.

Here is inscribed into the wood, vividly and clearly, inside a heart-shaped sculpt:

E + R
Together Forever
317 until 0116

And this is the meaning of their scription:

Three people, one team, and 7 years until no one is left to fulfill the one dream of 6 ages and forevermore:

Unity

"I couldn't have done it without you, y'know," Eddy admitted.

"Love, I must tell you something, that you may rest in wholesome peace. Eddy, you may not remember, but you were the father of a beautiful young man. He is so healthy and strong, like you.

"Eddy, about what you said with the memory chip... I am most appreciative, but this scene, as wonderful as it is, I must say it wasn't what I first imagined..." Eddy grinned in agreement.

He claps his hands twice. They appear in the hospital. Eddy is on the bed.

"My love, it is so, because, back then, it was I who was on the deathbed, and not you, Rebekah. I know this truth now, after fighting off some doubts.

"I had never known any truer love than you at my side through it all. When I died today, I was finally able to remember," said Eddy. They reappeared back in the beautiful world. Rebekah beams from ear to ear, for she has a secret to share with him.

"Your son is able to join us too, but only briefly. Do not worry, he is very much alive and well!" A figure appears with them. It is Macht?!

"Father!"

"M-Macht?! Is that you?"

"No, father, I am your son Isaac. I became a doctor, aren't you proud of me? You were never able to tell me in person anymore after you were drafted for your project. I was your surgeon for your brain operation. Mother was here, too. She was there for you until the very end. Father, she loved you so much. I couldn't have asked for a better set of parents.

"The brain damage you received was destroying your memory. I wanted to preserve it all for a moment such as this. I created the memory chip. The only problem was the Project.

"Macht and Okami were the names of your prototypes to use in the war. One day, a model fell on your head. Of which, we now know the cause being a former friend acting out of spite," said Isaac.

"Who exactly were Macht and Okami then in my dreams?" asked Eddy.

"From the notes we found on your desk, and I quote, they represented the best ideas of devastation you believed possible, given that they were originally intended as your model bombs. This helped in the operation because I had to use names you were familiar with, or it wouldn't have worked. Also, Yakeru was indeed your childhood friend and mentor in the real world, when your father would take you to visit the Nishimura's lab," replied Isaac.

"I remember now. He was so bright, a true candle lit with fiery passion for science. But as for the timeline, the places?" Eddy asked.

"I bridged together the times and places you knew best. Some logic had to be added so you would stay comatose during the surgery. You may have heard me ask you a couple questions along the way, whenever you whited out, so that I could pull you back in." said Malcolm.

"I understand. So why did I die after Macht?" Eddy asked, becoming unsettled for the answer he was afraid to hear.

"It wasn't Macht who died, Father. That was you, because I had finished the memory chip after a long operation of 52 hours. I did my best to make sure it was as painless as possible." He stopped a moment, eyes sombering and turning red. Isaac looked at his mother and father.

"This is the last moment I was able to give you, Father" said Isaac, his voice quivering.

"What was the meaning of it all?" asked Eddy.

"To fully pull your memory into the chip, I searched your memories all over for the one dream you wanted to see.

"You wanted to be the best soldier and finish your work on the battlefield, and you wanted to find my mother all over again just to tell her you love her. I am sorry for some of the events you had to witness—those were mere mistakes on my part—but I know this: you were the greatest soldier and father to have ever lived. And that is no mistake." Isaac's being disappeared from this reality.

Rebekah begins to fade away also.

"So this is it, my love. Our final goodbyes," said Rebekah.

Rebekah and Eddy fondly embraced.

"You were the best father, my love... my Eddy... I will continue to do my best," she said.

"I'd expect nothing less from the Baron Rogue," he winked.

The two lovers evanesced from this resplendent world.

EPILOGUE

Rebekah found herself sitting down inside her son's operating theater. It was only her, Dr. Isaac Malcolm, and the now-deceased body of Edward J. Malcolm in the room.

The computer made a final chime, signifying that the memory chip was complete, fully infused with everything his father had ever experienced, thought, imagined, or envisioned, within the limits of Eddy's own recallable memory and fantasies.

Isaac picked up the chip and intently enclosed it inside a square glass case, which was then placed inside a sturdy box-like receptacle that had a felt-lined mold specifically for the glass case. He handed the box to his mother. She set it on her lap, her hands fumbling over it with numb-like fidgeting.

"I was able to preserve everything. But during the searches and scans, Father made some interesting choices along the way, among other things, so it may not be fully accurate.

"I suppose, in its own regard, that also makes it error-free. No matter his decisions, however sporadic, his love for you remained firm and unchanged," said Isaac.

Rebekah looked up at her son, her mouth quivering and her eyes redder than red itself.

Isaac rested his hand on her shoulder, mouthing the words "I love you," in an effort to console her.

A week later came the day for Edward J. Malcolm to rest at last.

Rebekah was seated next to Isaac. As the eulogist gave the benediction and final respects, he invited a special guest onto the platform. This particular fellow, who held a certain level of charisma, meant a great deal to Eddy.

"At this time, I would like to invite to this pulpit a figure that Edward looked up to, one he called his own hero. Please, Dr. J. Robert Oppenheimer, we now warmly welcome you up here," said the eulogist.

Oppenheimer meekly collected himself and presented his own eulogy.

"Thank you. Truly, I am humbled to share on Dr. Malcolm's behalf. A few days ago, it came to my attention that our Eddy was the victim of a horribly tragic incident. His days with us were too few, indeed. Despite the offender's malice against him, there is no vanity in his remembrance and the work he has done for us. On this particular occasion, though unfortunate, I am rather pleased to announce to you that his work has given us all we need to satisfy our project, and he will go down in history as one of the greatest, most passionate scientists to have ever lived. Again, I do appreciate this opportunity to speak here today. With solemn grace, we survive this great man. May Dr. Malcolm rest in beloved peace, knowing his work is done."

The eulogist approached the pulpit once more.

"We here do take solace in your kind words, Dr. Oppenheimer. For the next portion of our last moments with Eddy, his own son Isaac has prepared something for us." He steps away, letting Isaac maneuver to the stand.

"To stand with me in solidarity, I would like our good friend Yakeru Nishimura, the Candle of the Western Village, to join me here," started Isaac.

Yakeru joined Isaac at the podium.

"It is with deepest honor to celebrate the life of Eddy with you all. He and I go way back to the days of when my father and his grandfather would build steam engines together. It introduced us to our love for engineering, and it only grew from there," shared Yakeru.

The funeral procession and speeches carried onward. Our Edward Malcolm was laid to rest. It could be seen on his tombstone the following engraving:

Edward James Malcolm, 1916 ~ 1943
Husband. Father. Scientist. Soldier. Friend.
317 until 0116 Unity

Next to his tombstone, to its very right, lay another. The kind soul here had the following letterhead:

Marshall Richard Armstrong, 1920 ~ Dec 7, 1941
Friend. Comrade. Hero.
Gone, Never Forgotten.
Ratiocinator Specialist of the 0116

After the final goodbyes, Yakeru and a friend of Rebekah privately went up to her.

"Hey Kathryn, Yakeru," said Rebekah tenderly.

"Hey there, darling," said Kathryn, going in for a side hug. "We have something for you."

Yakeru stepped forward and showed Rebekah a medallion made of polished gold.

"What is this?" asked Rebekah.

"Yakeru and I found this in Eddy's old lab. It seems like an unfinished project of sorts," said Kathryn. Rebekah noticed a hinge on it.

Upon opening it, she found a mold that oddly resembled the shape of the memory chip that Isaac gave her.

Rebekah removed the case from her coat pocket, opened it, and transferred Eddy's memory chip into the medallion. The medallion began to glow as though a light had been shone onto a diamond. Almost instinctively, Rebekah bound the medallion around her neck.

A cursive script now appeared letter by letter, which read plainly,

The Baron Rogue.

"Looks like it fits perfectly," said a grinning Kathryn.

"He chose wisely," added Yakeru.

After a couple sniffles and chuckles, Rebekah asked them, "When do we start?"

- The End -

AFTERWORD

On January 10, 2018, the idea of *The Baron Rogue* came to me one morning after an intense dream. Inside this dream, the world was suddenly different. My friends no longer knew who I was, nor I them. Unexplainably, we were all at war with each other for reasons unknown. All we knew is that everyone else had to die by any means possible. Towards the end of the dream, the restoration began. I begged and pleaded with my best friend to remember me. I knew we had a history together, it was there somewhere, buried deep in the archives of our minds.

Thus, *The Baron Rogue* was born. Macht, whose name translates to "Power," was born. He represented anxiety incarnate, the struggle for the peace and control over your own mind. Macht intimately knew that the battlefield was in Eddy's mind. There was no physical sign or symptom that could tell the internal war that rages on in the psyche. Eddy masked the anxiety all too well. He would fidget, gaslight himself, overthink often, and be consumed with anything but a positive thought.

If Macht, anxiety itself, could assume full control over Eddy's mind, then he could have everything he wanted. The whole world feared Macht because of his control. The moment you yielded to him, that is the end of the line for you.

Notice how Macht's methods against Eddy specifically were mainly psychological. Not necessarily trying to physically harm Eddy (yet), but to morally degrade him into dust.

We see the pressure of a deadline (one week), the constant threats, the desire to procrastinate, the scrambling of the mind. When the time came, he struggled to discern fantasy from reality because he could not accept reality.

Recall in Chapter VII that we finally see Eddy being locked into what is, essentially, and for all intents and purposes, a therapy session, albeit against his own will. Of course, this was a device used by Macht to obtain information in the process of creating his version of the memory chip. Every time Macht won against Eddy, Macht became stronger.

It was not until the very end that we saw Eddy go all-out against the anxiety that has troubled him all those years. The tricks, lies, and deceits no longer worked. Eddy was focused, determined. While it appears that Eddy was fully responsible for creating Macht (which was the case), I personally see it as his own introspective war being manifested.

Either way, it was surely not without consequence, keeping in mind what Macht said. Every action, imagination, decision, or thought was irreversible, for that was the memory to be on record. Isaac's version of the memory chip would reflect the same, as we saw him disclose that there were some inaccuracies on it due to Eddy's internal turmoil to accept what actually happened.

Truthfully, for Eddy to progress, he had to consciously make the choice to acknowledge his internal spars and take the steps necessary for overcoming them. Of course, without his stupendous support group, namely Kathryn and Rebekah and a few others, I am not sure how far Eddy would have gotten. And I believe all that is what makes the story so relevant.

Having help, and sometimes asking for it, did not make Eddy weak, or weaker, if you will, but rather propelled him into becoming the best version of himself: The Baron Rogue Proper.

Now to acknowledge the burning question: why did I choose the era of WWII as my setting?

I sought to envision what it must have felt like, to any degree, that adrenaline-pumping, heart-sinking moment a young person received his letter to be drafted. Following suit, I tried to empathize with the visions that soldiers would have before even going to war. More specifically, I wanted Eddy to remember the events at Pearl Harbor and to elaborate on them. I desired for him to confront his PTSD about it during the forced therapy session. It was the elephant-in-the-room, so to speak. He desperately tried to forget about it without ever trying to process it and let the thoughts pass freely. Talking through it was his personal way of finding peace about it, as we witnessed. I must disclaim to you now that discovering peace about a personal traumatic event may not always fully resolve. Macht experienced that himself.

To those who feel as if they may never experience a good night's rest again to such things, you are heard.

I believe the lesson we can learn from *The Baron Rogue* and his story is to at least try. Try to fight that good fight. This war is not yet over. It might not look pretty thus far. But you can change its outcome.

You can do it. Just like with Eddy's battles, it will not be a pleasant experience to fight through it, but it is worth the try. It will take grueling hardship and plenty of tears. You will feel like giving up. You mustn't. You are a tree that blooms under fire.

> *Give up? I shan't!*
> *Bloom? Darling, I shall!*
> Someone always cares.
> Do take care.

yours truly,
aaron.